HIGH RISE
Secrets

CARA WADE

First published Feburary 2021

Copyright © Cara Wade 2021

Published by Wade House Publishing

Cover design by Cara Wade

Developmental and copy editing provided by Kendra Gaither at Kendra's Editing and Book Services

For anyone who has yet to find their inner stripper...

INTRODUCTION

ADDISON

Rubble and ashes.

That's going to be the only thing left of the horrid place that's changed my life. The fire blazes hot, engulfing *The Devil's Playground*. Ironic that the devil's favorite element is the one to destroy this shitty club. This place—this hell I've been subjected to, along with my best friends, is gone, but we'll never forget.

Vince Perelli made it impossible for me to get a job anywhere, therefore confining me in his unbreakable cage. He forced me onto the stage, and forced me into private dances with his "clients." *Clients. What a load of shit.* The assholes that came to this shithole wanted scared girls to shove their dicks in for an easy, barely legal lay.

Now he's gone, just like the club, but I feel more trapped than ever. This place has been my life for only a short time, but I feel years older. The things I've seen—done here have aged me. Maybe not physically, but mentally. I'm no longer a lost nineteen-year-old looking for a fresh start after losing her family.

This place has brought out the nympho inside me, and as much as I hate to admit it, I'm scared of not having an outlet to unleash my inner goddess. I fear she'll be my destruction if she can't be tamed.

We all lost something in the fire. I lost *hope*. Isn't that fucked up? After all the shit I've dealt with in my life, this place was finally giving me hope for the future. It's where I met *him*. It's where I decided what I wanted in my life and the path I wanted to take.

"Okay, don't freak... just hear me out, okay?" Eden's soft voice breaks through my tunnel vision as I watch the building burn to the ground. "We should take all this money and open our own club."

What? Why the hell would we want to open a sleazy strip club again? What benefit would there be to that?

"What?" Magnolia mirrors my own thoughts. "Eden, we just... how... why would you wanna do that?"

"It doesn't have to be anything like Vince's place. It can be... different." Eden's voice is strong now. She knows this is what she wants, and she wants us to be part of it—her sisters.

Different.

The word feels heavy on my tongue as I try it out on a whisper to myself. How could a strip club be different? Disgusting men come to these places to jack off as they watch pretty girls take off their clothes.

"Different how?" Lia asks, looking at Everleigh and me, searching for support.

"How ever we want." Eady shrugs. "It'll be ours. Ours to run, as equal owners. A place where we can have our freedom, a safe haven for little birdies like we were."

I'm trying to fast track my MBA, taking five classes each semester, along with summer classes. I can read about running a business all I want, but what better way to learn than by doing? Real life experience has its perks.

I look to Lia, and she gives Eady a smile that's not quite as sad as the ones she normally wears. All she's ever wanted to do was dance, to be free of her shitty husband and shitty family. She was dragged into this life without much of a choice.

"We don't have to strip if we don't wanna," Lia blurts out. "And we don't have to... we don't have to do *anything* with any of the men if we don't wanna either." There is a spark of life in her eyes I haven't seen before. She's in. Even without her saying the words yet, I know she's made her decision.

I look to Everleigh, who is aghast. She's going to be the hardest one of all of us to win over. She's always been the ice queen, the hardest to crack. She's dealt with a lot of teasing and has built up her walls to protect herself. She's going to fight us on this, but in the end, I know she'll be on board. She'll never turn her back on her sisters, even if she has to stab someone in the process.

And me? Well, Eden's idea offers me hope. How can I turn my back on that?

PROLOGUE

ADDISON- VALENTINE'S DAY

I slide into the booth where my sisters, my best friends, are waiting for me. It's an annual tradition for us girls to spend Valentine's Day together. We always book a table at one of the fanciest restaurants around the city and spend the night drinking and laughing.

After, I usually head over to *RISE* and find some lonely stud to take to bed and play with him until I've had no less than three orgasms. He's always more willing to please on Valentine's Day, trying to be romantic and shit. It doesn't bother me in the slightest; they usually try harder.

What does bother me? Ethan Freeman's date for the evening. She's his flavor of the month and annoying as hell. Her laugh? Ugh, like nails on a chalkboard. She must have a magical vagina or something because I can't figure out what he sees in her. Oh, and he happens to be in the same restaurant we're at.

Coincidence?

Never. I set up his reservation last week for him and wanted to keep an eye on him.

"Lia, so glad Landry gave you up for the evening. Was he a sad panda?" I ask, taking a sip of my appletini.

"He told me he has a special evenin' planned when I get home." Her eyes sparkle with love as she talks about her husband. They make me sick but in a loving way.

I look at Everleigh, who smirks at me, daring me to say something about her not being with Luca tonight. I see her hand twitch with the need to give me a witty comeback or whip out her butterfly knife. I love the girl, and she is loyal to a fault, but she's a stabby bitch through and through.

"Hi, Ev, glad you could make it tonight." I blow her an air kiss over the table.

"Wouldn't miss this night for the world. One question, though." She places her hands under her chin and gives me a chilling smile. "What the fuck is Ethan Freeman doing here?" She flicks her chin in his direction.

I feel my cheeks heat as I turn to look in the direction she's motioned to. "Oh, is he? I didn't realize." My eyes lock with his over his date's shoulder, and he smirks at me. I wave a few fingers and turn in my seat again.

"Girl, I love you, but you need to move on. Clearly, he hasn't seen what's right in front of him after all these years. You're amazing, and he's a dumb fuck."

I chortle and choke on my drink as I roll my eyes at her. She's not wrong, but I'd never admit that to her. My *slight* obsession with my boss is my cross to bear. "Hey, Eady, how're you doing?"

"Fine. Happy to be here with you girls tonight." She bumps her shoulder against mine as we all settle in with drinks and order a few appetizers.

The conversation is flowing as are the alcohol and food. This is the only way to spend a shitty holiday made popular by greeting card companies—with my girls. I feel his eyes on me though, and I can't help but turn around just in time to see his date storm off, taking her purse with her.

"Doubt she's just running to the bathroom," Ev says, hiding her smirk behind her hand. Ethan is a statue of calm as he takes a sip of his drink, eyes glued to our table. A few patrons at the tables close by are watching him, but he doesn't even seem to notice them.

"I need to go check on him, make sure he's okay," I mumble as I slide out of the booth.

"You're gonna ditch your girls for dick?" Ev asks, shaking her head. If she didn't have a smile on her face, I'd think she was mad at me.

"Chicks before dick, Addy," Eady chimes in.

"You know how much I like dick, and that one is my filet mignon. Just for a minute, I'll be back," I reason with them.

I know it's a lie as soon as my eyes lock with his gorgeous brown ones. He waves me over to the table, and like a willing lamb, I gravitate to the big bad wolf. Ethan Freeman will always be my ultimate, even if he has no clue of our past and who I really am.

ETHAN

I knew this date was a mistake the moment Addison fucking Snyder walked in and sat down at a booth three tables away. Yes, I've counted just how fucking close she is to me, and I'm sure I'm imagining it, but I can smell her signature scent from here.

Brittany, my date, returns from the restroom and flashes a megawatt smile until she sees me staring at Addison's table. Brittany looks over her shoulder to see who I smiled at and turns back to me, her eyes narrowed. "Who's that?" she asks, crossing her arms, resting them on the table.

"My assistant," I reply, taking a sip of my drink.

Did Addison make this reservation knowing she was going to be here, too?

Don't be an idiot, Ethan.

Tatalina is one of the fanciest restaurants in town and hard as fuck to get a reservation at. I knew when I asked her to get me a table somewhere tonight, she would come through. She always does. Nothing more.

The waiter comes over just in time to avoid a disaster that's waiting to happen. Pretty girls like Brittany are all the same, in my experience anyway. If there is another woman who's caught my eye, she gets jealous. We place our orders, and I distract her by asking about work and the charity work she's involved in.

The evening seems to be dragging on, and I've barely said two words to her, my focus on the table three spots away. Thank God Addison isn't facing me. I wouldn't be able to pretend to be enjoying this date if she was.

"Brittany, this was a mistake," I cut her off as she drones on about the latest gossip in her social circle. I wince at the bite of my words. I sound like the biggest asshole, and I know she's going to cause a scene.

She scoffs and grabs her purse. "A mistake?" she seethes. "You're right, this isn't working out. Fuck you, Ethan." She stands and storms away from the table. A few people are looking at us, but I don't care. I only care when Addison turns to look at me, and I motion her over to the table. When she willingly stands and saunters over to me, I feel like the luckiest man alive.

"Ms. Snyder," I say coolly as I point to the empty seat in front of me.

"Mr. Freeman, it appears you lost your date for the evening."

"I have. I'd love it if you'd join me." She glances back at her friends and bites her lip. I lower my voice. "Don't make me beg, Addy. I just lost my date for the night. Show a guy some mercy on Valentine's Day." *Oh yeah, I'm laying it on thick.* I take a moment to appreciate her amazing body before she smiles and sits.

"To see a big bad CEO beg, that would be a sight to behold."

"Deny me, and I'll have no option."

Her smile widens and I catch a mischievous glint in her green eyes. I wonder where her mind just wandered to. *Does she think about me the same way I think about her?* Unlikely.

"I can't stay too long, I have a date in a little bit," she says.

"Well then, he's one lucky guy to have caught your attention. Just stay with me long enough to have a drink, and then I'll let you get back to your friends. I don't want to keep you."

She reaches across the table, placing her small hand on top of mine. My flesh buzzes where her hand is, and it takes everything in me not to trap her against me by covering her hand with my own. "You're not. I wanted to make sure you were okay. Brittany ran out of here so fast."

"Yeah, well, she caught me staring at a pretty girl."

She pulls her hand back. "Oh, well, why isn't she sitting here then?"

She is. Not that I can tell her that. I can't date my assistant, no matter how much I want her.

CHAPTER 1

ADDISON

M y feet are killing me from all the running around I've done today. I haven't figured out why normal high heels are so uncomfortable, yet stripper heels I can stand in all night and not fuss at all. *Go figure.* I push my dark hair over my shoulder and review Mr. Freeman's schedule again.

The light in his office is still on. I glance at the time on the corner of the screen and huff in annoyance. It's already half past seven. This man sure does like to burn the midnight oil. He's been like this ever since I started at *Emulation* five years ago. Mr. Freeman is the owner and CEO of the company. He took over two years ago from his father. Don't let that fool you though; he is one of the hardest workers I know and deserves it all. Nepotism only goes so far with him.

When I started here, I was an assistant to one of the developers and have worked my way through the ranks. While I'm lucky to have received the position, I also worked my ass off to get it. Mr. Freeman's old executive assistant quit a year ago—something about his being too demanding and the job being too hard.

That's the story circulating, anyway. Apparently, Janice, his old assistant, wanted to sleep with him. So, instead of concentrating on her job and helping make his life easier, she paraded herself around here trying to catch his eye. She caught it all right, especially when he walked in on her pleasuring herself at his desk one night after she thought he was gone.

Stupid girl... everyone knows you use the bathroom if you're going to do that.

How do I know this, you might ask? I'm good friends with Aiden in human resources, and I may have gotten him drunk one night and dragged the information out of him. It doesn't help that I gave him a lap dance and promised to get him off if he told me. Easiest night of my life. I can do that move in my sleep; I've been doing it for so long.

That makes me sound horrible, doesn't it? Let me take you back a ways. I have an alter ego as Madam Ember at the gentleman's club *RISE* outside of Atlanta. I got my start at *The Devil's Playground*, which was in a shady part of town and owned by an even shadier man before it burned to the ground with him in it.

Nine years ago, my girls and I decided to open *RISE* as a way to allow women to support and protect themselves. Best decision of my life. I get all the sex I want while knowing I won't get killed in the process. The club is half the reason I wanted to get my MBA. The other half is the man I work for.

"Addy, can you come here for a second?" The deep timbre of his voice sends a chill down my spine. I could listen to him talk all day and never get bored. I stand and flinch as my shoe pinches my baby toe. *Son of a bitch!* For eight-hundred dollars, these Jimmy Choo's should feel like I'm walking on clouds. Note to self, bring extra shoes next time.

I smooth out my skirt and step into his oversized office. The shades are drawn, blocking out the darkened city view behind him. He's wearing a pair of navy chinos, a crisp white shirt with the top two buttons undone, and his hair is styled to perfection. Even under tremendous stress, his appearance is pristine.

Memories of the amazing sex we had so many years ago infiltrate my mind, and I try to pull my thoughts back before I get myself in trouble.

"What can I help you with, Mr. Freeman?"

He glances over at me from his laptop screen. I hold the tablet in my hand, waiting for whatever instructions he's going to give. "Have a seat."

I smooth the back of my skirt under my butt and sit in the chair he motions to, crossing my legs over one another. He leans back and steeples his fingers under his chin. I study his features for a little longer than necessary, taking in his deep brown eyes, his perfectly coiffed chestnut hair, and strong jaw. My mind wanders, and I imagine running my fingers through his hair, tugging him closer to me.

I seriously need to get laid tonight. Madam Ember is going to be on the prowl...

"I have a meeting with Clyde Willows tomorrow. I want you to cancel it." His words pull me from my inappropriate fantasy.

"Okay, and the reason I should tell his office?" I pull up an email to draft it. I know Clyde isn't in the office at this time. He's probably over at *RISE* for the night, enjoying one of the girls' shows. I'm very familiar with Clyde and his habitual habits.

"I have a conflicting appointment and need to reschedule."

I smirk. He knows I know his schedule inside and out. I glance up into his dark eyes that are dancing with amusement. "And the real reason? For my knowledge."

He sits forward, resting his forearms on his desk. "I don't

like how he handles business and don't want to associate myself with him."

His eyes stay locked on mine, and I fight the urge to lick my suddenly dry lips. My phone rings in my lap, and I jump to turn the ringer off. "Sorry," I mumble, hitting the ignore button.

"Popular tonight, aren't you?" His face is stoic, but I can tell he's amused.

"I'm supposed to be at my friend's wedding dinner party. She got married a few weeks ago in a surprise ceremony, but wanted to have a small, formal celebration with her friends and family. It started half an hour ago."

He raises his brow and runs his fingers along the stubble that has grown since his shave this morning. Watching him stroke his chin is erotic and so wrong. I know I shouldn't think of my boss that way, but there aren't many thirty-one-year-olds that look and act like him. He could be a model—he has the whole package—yet he has the brains, too. And I know for a *fact* he's a giver. Both inside the bedroom and out.

"So, what are you still doing here then?" His voice is low and beyond sexy.

I chuckle and shake my head, a few loose wisps framing my face. "You're here." Those two words hold more meaning behind them than he will ever know. "My job isn't done for the night until you leave."

"Get out of here, Addy. Enjoy your night. You don't want to end up like me—a workaholic." He undocks his laptop and starts cleaning up his desk. "Besides, you're right. I should head home."

I stand and offer him a smile. "Okay then. Enjoy your night, Mr. Freeman."

He shakes his head and looks down at his desk. "How many times do I have to ask you to call me Ethan?"

I shrug my shoulders and step out of his office without another word. I open a new message and send it to Lia.

Me: *I know, I'm coming. I got stuck at work. I'm running out the door now. Tell Ev to put her shanks away.*

I toss my phone into my purse and pack my things at record speed. Walking to the front of the office, I press the button on the elevator and wait as I watch the numbers light up one by one. Ethan steps up behind me, and we both walk in. He stands in one corner, and I stand in the other.

His cologne tickles my nose as the small space fills with his scent. My pulse flutters frantically, and I shift my weight, trying to ward off the need pulsing between my legs. *What is it about damn elevators?* He moves his hands discreetly in front of him, and it takes all my human strength not to look down.

One little peek wouldn't hurt, right?

I remember what he's packing down there, and it's a hell of a lot. My cheeks flush at the thought of our romp all those years ago—not that he would remember. I was just a stripper, a faceless girl. I take a shallow breath and try to stop my fluttering heart.

The doors slide open, and I rush out into the parking garage in a hurry to get to my car. He calls out to me, wishing me a good night, but I barely register it as I slide into my black Audi. He's just reached his car as I drive past and offer a wave as I rush to get to the restaurant.

I pull up to the valet in no less than ten minutes and toss him the keys as I all but run inside with the gift I bought for Everleigh and Luca. I can't believe she's married and has an adoptive daughter, Aurora, who we call Rory for short. I never thought this day would come, not with everything that seemed to be working against them. Luca is a good guy though, and the two of them couldn't be more perfect for one another.

Especially because if he does anything to hurt her, he's going to have to deal with us three girls, and he has seen what happens when we work together. Needless to say, he's screwed if he ever tries to go against us.

I meet eyes with Eden first, and she gives me 'the look'. *Yeah, yeah, I know I'm late.* I may be a few months older than her, but she still acts like a mother hen. I wouldn't change her for the world, though. She protected me and the other girls when no one else would, and I'm thankful for it. Without her, I wouldn't be part owner of *RISE*.

I look around the table at my friends and smile at the small family I found on my own. Everleigh finally notices me, jumps up from the table, and envelops me in a hug.

"Sorry I'm late," I say, squeezing her back. She pulls away, and I hold the bag out in front of me for her to take. "Congrats on finally tying the knot. Luca is a lucky man."

"Fuck yes, I am, and I know it, too," Luca chimes in.

Ev blushes but rolls her eyes at him. "I'll cut a bitch if he ever tries anything stupid again." She glances over at him as he holds their daughter protectively in his arms. "Ethan at the office late again?"

I nod and smile at her. "That man would work through the night if he could." I wave my hands in front of me, dismissing the thought. "Anyway, I'm here now, and I need a drink and some time with my girls."

I make my way around the table, stopping to give Landry a hug from behind. I smack a wet kiss on his cheek, and then move to Lia, doing the same to her and her adorable daughter, Aliana, who wiggles in her highchair.

"Gross, Addy," she chuckles as she wipes the wetness from her cheek.

"Hey, people pay good money for my spit. Don't wipe it off," I whisper to her.

She shakes her head and makes starry eyes at her husband again. *Those two are in their own little bubble.*

Eden stands with her hands on her hips, waiting for me to make it over to her. "You're late, bitch," she says.

"I know. You know how demanding Ethan is." She raises her eyebrow in question, and I roll my eyes. "Not like that. I mean, he was when we were younger, so I bet he still is now." I give her my best sultry smirk until she finally laughs.

I wave hello to Everleigh and Luca's families as I put my stuff down and walk over to the bar. *This girl needs some liquor.*

I place my order, but not before flirting with the bartender. He's cute. He might be a fun hook-up for the night, and since Ethan got my panties all wet with his sexiness today, there is no reason I can't use someone else as a replacement.

Eden joins me, and when I smile looking at the happy couple, she scowls. She orders a drink, and as I wait for the bartender to make them, I turn to look at the table of people again.

I knock my elbow into Eden. "Hey, what's wrong?"

She shakes her head, her dark curls flowing around her shoulders. "Nothing. I'm fine."

The bartender puts our drinks on the table. I give him a wink and look at his number on the cocktail napkin. Eden glances down and rolls her eyes.

I choose to ignore her gesture and continue. "Well, I guess it's just the two of us flying solo now. We gotta stick together." I bump my hip against hers and take a sip of my drink. *Damn, he made a good Cosmo.*

"Guess so," she says, sounding dejected. She watches the table of everyone laughing and having a good time, but it's like she's seeing them as strangers, not our family.

"Come on, Eady, smile. I was thinking of heading to the club after this to let off some steam anyway. Wanna come?"

She sighs but declines with a head shake. She walks ahead of me, and I turn back to the bartender, cocking my finger in his direction. I lean over the bar, giving him a view down the front of my blouse. I hand him a gold *RISE* card with Madam Ember scribbled on the back. "Ask at the front and show them this card." *It's been a long few days, and I'm craving something yummy.* Since I can't have my boss, Mister Flirty Eyes will have to do.

Until then, I re-join everyone at the table to celebrate Everleigh and Luca's newest adventures as husband and wife.

CHAPTER 2

ETHAN

Addy runs out of the elevator so fast I swear I have whiplash. Thank God the elevator ride wasn't longer. It was hard enough to conceal what she does to me without her picking up on it. Last thing I need is some sexual harassment suit because I can't control my own dick. Imagine the headlines. *Young CEO can't keep it in his pants.* I'm sure every client would drop me like flies.

Addison Snyder makes me crazy, especially when she says my name. *Ethan.* The way it rolls off her tongue is sinful. She's an angel made by the Devil himself, sent here to tempt me. Too bad I can't get her to say it more often. *Especially as I pound into her, bringing her to climax.* She's so stuck on this damn Mr. Freeman shit. The only time I've heard her call me Ethan is when she didn't know I was listening. She was talking to a friend about me, and I could have sworn she said my name on a sigh—like she was fantasizing about me. That also could be wishful thinking on my part.

She's never been anything but completely professional with me, and after the Janice incident, I should be thankful. Addy swooped in like a saint and took over, keeping me on track. *Not that I can't keep my own time, but damn is she good at her job.* One of the best hiring decisions I've made by far.

When she started at *Emulation*, I knew it was a matter of time before she either moved through the ranks or left. She needs a challenge, so when I was finally able to kick Janice to the curb, I made HRs life hell until she was my assistant. Unlike my father, I've spent a lot of time making sure I know who is working for me. I can't trust who I don't know.

She comes in every day wearing those fuck-me heels and skirts that make my cock ache. The number of fantasies I've had of bending her over my desk and fucking her until we're both sweaty messes is unreal. I readjust myself and shake the thoughts from my head, clicking the unlock button on my FOB. I get into my car and sit there for a minute.

I've been working late a few nights a week, simply so I can spend some time with her. I know if I wait long enough, no one else will be in the office. That means as long as she doesn't run too fast, we can take the elevator down together. Every time I step in after her, she straightens her spine and keeps her eyes forward, then runs as fast as her heeled feet will take her.

Which, by the way, is fast. I've never known a woman who can run in heels like she can.

I turn on my car and leave to go home. I know Rhoda, my housekeeper, will have put something in the fridge for me, but the thought of having another meal alone is unappealing. I could go to a restaurant, but don't want people gawking as I eat alone. I definitely don't want some waitress hitting on me again, either. That's how my last relationship started. Turns out my money was the only thing she was after...

My phone rings, and David, a friend from college's name displays on my car dash.

"Hey, man, what's going on?" I ask, trying to sound happy

he's calling. I haven't seen or heard from David in about five years. Last I heard, he got some girl knocked up and she was making him tie the knot.

"Hey, man, long time no talk. I'm in town and wanted to know if you wanted to hit some of the clubs like we did when we were younger. You know, relive the glory days?" he chuckles into the phone.

"Don't you have a wife and kids or some shit now? Are you sure she approves?" I joke.

"Kid yes, wife no. I love my boy to death, but he's with his mom and I'm in town for business for a few days. I wanted to kick off some steam. Maybe we can visit a strip club. Is that one we went to years ago still around? What was the name? *Devil's Hotspot* or some shit? You know, that place where you had amazing sex with that stripper?"

Ember.

I haven't thought about her since Addison became my assistant. There was something so innocent about her that I couldn't help requesting a private show when I watched her on stage. I expected her to dance for me, maybe go as far as a hand job, but she did so much more than that. I had to get out of the room and out of the club that night before I went back and demanded that she leave with me.

What I wouldn't give to see the look on Dad's face if I came home with a stripper. Fucking hilarious.

"*The Devil's Playground.* That burned down years ago. There's a new place that opened a few years ago called *RISE.* I think a group of women own it." *RISE* is the only strip club left in town, but I haven't stepped foot in it. Last time I had the chance was when I was working with my buddy Landry Laurent, but even then, I sent someone in my place to work the deal.

"Women, huh? Kinky fucks." He laughs at his own joke and

I roll my eyes. "For old times' sake, wanna go? We can meet there at nine-thirty or so? Give the place a chance to really come alive."

"Sure, what have I got to lose?" Maybe a lap dance will help me forget all about the sexy assistant that keeps me hard all day long.

I PULL UP OUTSIDE THE CLUB. IT'S A HELL OF A LOT NICER THAN the shithole I was at with David last time. David approaches me, and we give each other a high-five shake as we walk to the front door. The bouncer outside has a clipboard.

"Name?" he asks.

Is there a special event going on or something? "Ethan Freeman."

The bouncer looks up at me, squinting his eyes like he doesn't believe it, but puts a check next to my name. "Keep your guest in line."

What the fuck is he talking about? "Ah, okay. Thanks." Why the hell am I on a list here, anyway? I've never even stepped foot in the place. I shrug it off and push through the heavy metal door.

The bass beats around us, and there is a girl who looks no older than eighteen spinning around the pole. *Jesus, she looks like a kid!* I take in the other patrons in the room, most of whom have their eyes glued to the girl on stage. A few girls roam around the room with trays of drinks in their hands, and a few more sit in the laps of other men, giggling. All of them are wearing masks and colorful wigs.

This place is nice as hell. I guess I was expecting it to be like the old strip club, rundown and dirty. The booths are classy and not patched with duct tape, the floor isn't sticky, and the girls actually look happy to be here. I look at the stage as the girl finishes her set and collects the bills thrown at her.

Yep. Still in a strip club.

"Let's grab a seat by the stage. Maybe even help a poor girl out and give her a little extra if she rubs me just right," David says, elbowing me in the stomach in his excitement.

Now, I remember the reason I didn't give this asshole a job with me. He thinks the world belongs to him and people should bow down at his feet. I'm starting to regret my decision to come here with him.

I look around and lock eyes with a girl who smiles bashfully and waves at me from across the room. She definitely knows what she wants, and I'm not the one to give it to her tonight. I ignore her and motion to a girl with a tray.

"Can I get a Jack and Coke?"

David orders something, too, and the girl scurries off. I don't need a private dance tonight. *No, I need Addy willing to do all sorts of naughty stuff with me.* The thought of her makes me hard again, and I adjust myself. Fuck. Maybe I *could* use a private dance after all. It might be nice to give my right hand a break.

Let me get one thing straight. I can get as much action as I want. Women fawn over me because of my damn money, and I'm not bad on the eyes either. I know that. I spend a lot of time with my personal trainer to keep my physique in top shape. The problem is, all these women become faceless. I want a night with someone who doesn't know me as Ethan Freeman, Atlanta's youngest CEO and runner-up for bachelor of the year. *I still think I should have won the honors, but what can you do.*

The girl returns with our drinks, and I place a fifty-dollar bill on her tray and tell her to keep the change. Her eyes light up as she turns to leave us alone. David is talking about his job or some shit; I'm not really listening to him. I'm looking around for *Ember*. It would be silly to think she still works at a strip club after all these years.

Don't most strippers last a few years and move on? She probably has a good job and is settled down now with a couple of kids and a nice husband. Most of the girls working here seem to be in their late teens to mid-twenties. Ember has to be somewhere close to thirty at this point.

I look around and notice a girl with long red hair leading a man toward the back room. She looks back at him with a smile on her face, and I catch her eye, but only for a moment. My heart races inside my chest, and I stand abruptly. A sense of déjà vu washes over me as I focus my attention on the couple.

I know that smile. Jesus, that girl looks so familiar.

"Dude, what's wrong?" David asks, drawing my attention back to him. I turn to look at him as the mystery girl disappears down a hallway.

"Nothing. I'll be right back." I leave my drink and head in the direction my mystery girl went. A large man steps in my way, blocking my path. He crosses his arms over his chest and glares at me.

"Who was that girl?"

"One of the owners," he grunts.

"I need her name, please." I'm fucking desperate for information. I run my fingers through my hair and try to look past the hulking giant standing in my way to catch another glimpse of her.

"Unless you're paying, and she's accepted the offer, you don't need to know. Either go back to your seat or leave."

I put my hands up in surrender. I don't need to risk getting kicked out of here or causing a scene. I'll find out about this place and who owns it if it's the last thing I do.

CHAPTER 3

ADDISON

So, hottie bartender wasn't as good in the sack as I thought he would be. His dick was a decent size, but he clearly has never been shown where a woman's clitoris is located. I spent my time trying to wriggle around until he could find it, then gave him fake praise when he managed to skirt over it. Ultimately, though, I had to do it myself. *Especially because he came in under two minutes.*

I'm sitting in the small office looking over the list of clients who have come in for the night. Mostly, it's the same men who are here weekly, but I stop scrolling down the list and gasp when I see Ethan's name. I have looked over this list every night since opening, hoping to see his name. Every night has been the same disappointment—until now.

I stand, fix my mask in place, and walk out onto the main floor. My eyes scan the crowd looking for the one man who makes me weak in the knees and turns my insides into jelly. The place is mostly cleared out, with it being one in the morning, but I hoped to see him. I see Washington, our bouncer, who was on door duty tonight and walk up to him, draping my arm over his large forearm.

"Hi, sexy," I coo. I just like to flirt with the man, not that I need to. "Ethan Freeman was here tonight. Do you know what time he left?" I rub my barely covered breast over his arm, and he looks down at me, a tiny smirk gracing his lips.

"No, ma'am. I think it was shortly after your friend for the evening arrived."

I roll my eyes. *Once again, poor choice on my part.* "Yeah, if you see my friend," I say, putting air quotes around the word, "come around again, please don't let him in unless he wants a membership." He nods once in understanding. "Thanks, hon. I'm going to head out. Have a good night." I pull him down and smack a kiss on his cheek.

"Have a good night, Madam Ember." I watch him discreetly touch his cheek and smile to myself. That man is such a softy underneath his rock-like body. He would do anything for us girls.

I walk to the locker room to take my mask and wig off. Then I change into my clothes from work that day and leave through the back door. My black Audi is tucked toward the back of the lot, and I click the FOB to unlock the doors, checking the backseat before I get in. A girl can never be too careful. The ride home is silent, but my mind has been reeling. Why did he show up after all this time?

"Addy, what the hell is this?" Eden asked, shaking a piece of paper in front of my face.

"A sheet of paper?" I responded coyly and went back to looking at the books. We needed to bring in new clients if we were going to be able to keep this place growing. I'd been trying to come up with new ideas on how to entice new clientele.

"Why the fuck are Ethan Freeman's yearly dues being paid by you?"

I snapped my head to look at her, guilt written all over my face. I'd never been an exceptionally great liar, especially around those I love. There's no way she could have uncovered that information unless she was looking for it.

I opened my mouth to say something just as she cut me off. "Don't you fucking lie to me, Addy," *she seethed.*

Lia and Everleigh stepped into the small office. "Keep your voices down. We don't want the clients to hear. What's with all the ruckus? Whose balls am I ripping off?" *Everleigh asked.*

"Addison is so hung up on this fucking Ethan guy that she's paying his dues. I checked. He hasn't stepped foot in this club since we opened a few years ago," *Eden said, her arms crossed over her chest.*

"Seriously, Addy? Why are you so hung up on this guy anyway? Sure, he was a good lay, but he has no clue who you are," *Lia piped in.*

I stood and glared at my three best friends. I love them, but there were times when I wanted to wring their necks. "Fuck all of you. What I do with my money is my business. If I want to pay someone's dues, I'll pay them."

"All you're ever going to be to him is some random stripper he hooked up with. Jesus, Addy, he doesn't even know your real name. You told him your name was Ember. You don't have a chance in hell with that man. Until he actually comes to the club, I'm removing him from the list." *Eden slammed the paper down on the desk, and I glared at her.*

"Watch it, Eden," *I kept my voice low and stalked toward her.* "You have a lot of secrets yourself, and I would hate for some of them to come out." *She clenched her jaw but didn't say anything.* "He's staying on the list, and you're going to keep your nose out of my Goddamn business." *I glared between all of the girls.* "All of you are going to forget this, got it?"

"How do we even know he's safe? We can't have someone in here that hasn't been vetted," *Eden said.*

"I've done enough research on him. He's safe. The worst thing about him is his choice in dates." I mumbled the last part.

I stare at my building for a few minutes, replaying that night five years ago. Way before I got the job as Ethan's assistant. It's late, I'm tired, and I should go to bed. Thank God tomorrow is Saturday and I have nothing planned.

My phone buzzes next to me, and I look at the text from Ethan.

Ethan: *Sorry to text so late. I'm going to need you for a few hours tomorrow. Also, I need you to go to the charity ball with me next weekend. I'm trying to work a deal with a client and was invited last minute. I could really use you there. See you tomorrow morning.*

I know there's no use texting him back. He knows I'll show up. I put my stuff down in my apartment, kick off my shoes, and peel off the day's outfit. I take a quick shower and then go to bed where I fall asleep with images of Ethan and his fine ass body.

I ARRIVE AT THE OFFICE WITH TWO COFFEES IN HAND AT NINE-thirty. I take the elevator up, and when the doors slide open, my breath hitches. He's standing there in a pair of dark wash jeans, a fitted t-shirt, and his hair is messy chic, per usual. *Is there any look this man can't pull off?*

"You're late."

I hold a cup of coffee out for him, and he nods his thanks before taking a sip. "I'm not late. You never told me what time to come in, and since it is supposed to be a day off, I didn't think it mattered," I sass.

A tiny smirk graces his lips as he turns and walks into his

office. I roll my eyes, but follow, pulling my tablet out before taking a seat in my usual spot.

"So, the reason I asked you here. I need help trying to win over Patrick Hughes. Word is he's looking for a new company to partner with to handle internal security for his systems. I want the account."

I type Patrick Hughes into the search bar and look for basic information about him and his company. Not bad. Worth one-point-one million and his company has grown from ten employees to over one hundred in just a year. That's a huge growth in a short time.

Letting out a small whistle in interest, I ask, "Any idea why he needs it?" before taking a sip of my coffee. When he doesn't answer right away, I look up at him. He's staring at me, his lips parted slightly. I have the strongest urge to climb over his desk, sit in his lap, and kiss the look off his face.

Jesus, I really need to stop this.

I lick a drop of coffee off my lower lip and slowly pull my tongue back. He clears his throat. "Sorry." He mumbles something under his breath that I can't understand and starts again. "My understanding is he's had a few hacks and doesn't think his company's current security is working well." He smirks and I know exactly what he's up to. I've been working for him for long enough now. I know his signs. He's been the one hacking into their systems.

I smirk in return. "You're playing a dirty game, Mr. Free-man." *I want to play all sorts of dirty games with you.*

"Since we're on off-hours, how about you call me Ethan?"

"As long as I'm in this office, working," I raise an eyebrow in his direction, "I'll continue to call you Mr. Freeman. I can contact Mr. Hughes' office on Monday and request a meeting be set up."

He nods in approval. "Addy, this isn't going to be easy. I'm going to need all the help I can get to win this account. You've been able to get me meetings with everyone so far, and I know you won't let me down."

I stand and take my tablet with me. I know from past accounts he's won, it's going to take a lot of schmoozing on my part to make it happen, including a visit or two to *RISE*. Madam Ember is going to have to come out and play.

"Hey, Addy?" I stop in the doorway and turn to face him. "Do you know anything about *RISE*?"

CHAPTER 4

ETHAN

Addy looks like she's seen a ghost as soon as I ask her about the strip club. I jump up from my seat and rush to her side, hoping she's not going to faint like it appears. I place my firm hands on her delicate shoulders, and her skin warms my hands through the thin fabric.

I direct her to my seat, then squat in front of her, looking into her green eyes. Hers dart back and forth between my deep brown ones, and I know she's searching for something. God, she smells amazing like always. Without her usual heels, I have at least a solid foot on her. My mind wanders. There are so many fun, dirty things I could do with a girl so petite.

"Isn't it the strip club downtown?"

"Yes. It is." I stay silent and wait for her to say more. It's my signature move. Silence makes people uncomfortable, and they feel they have to fill the void. It's the best way to get a read on people and what they know. Stay silent for long enough and the truth always comes out.

"Why would I know anything about it?"

"I've been looking into it. Turns out I have a membership I

know nothing about, and I didn't know if you've happened to see invoices come across my desk. None have gone to my house."

Her whole body relaxes and she pushes out a shaky breath. *Strange.* "No. I haven't seen anything like that. Have you checked with Bill in accounting?"

"No," I say, dragging the word out a bit. It had to have been my father. He was always into the old-school way of doing business—sex and alcohol. "Sorry I asked."

We both stand at the same time, and the top of her head only comes to my mid-chest. *Jesus, she is tiny next to me.* I start to reach my hand out to her but pull it back at the last second. I need to get a grip. Addison is driving me insane. I can't even keep my damn erection at bay around her anymore. I turn to look at the window. "Thanks for coming in. Get that meeting set up and get me anything you think will help us win the bid. I'll see you on Monday."

I don't have to glance back at her to know I hurt her feelings by dismissing her. I mentally shake my head and berate myself for being a class-A asshole.

"H-have a good weekend, Mr. Freeman. See you on Monday. I'll call Mr. Hughes' office first thing on Monday and have an appointment made for you, and get some information and leave it on your desk."

I nod without looking at her, and when I hear the office door click into place again, I pull my phone from my pocket and dial dear old Dad's number. He answers on the first ring.

"Ethan, you haven't called me in ages. What do I owe the pleasure?"

"Did you purchase a membership at *RISE* for me?" I have a feeling the moment the words are out of my mouth, I know the answer.

"*I* can't even get a damn membership. What makes you think I bought one for you?"

Hmm, that's interesting.

"Why not?"

"No idea. I tried for years and was always denied. No way it's as good as Vince Perelli's place, though. I heard these girls actually fight back. Shame, really."

Fucking asshole. I am going to have to do some research on this. Someone has to be paying my dues if I'm on the damn list. Who the hell would be paying for them though? Looks like my weekend will be spent digging through records and information. "Thanks anyway, Dad." I try to hang up and he stops me.

"Since you have a membership, how about you help your old man out and invite me there one night. It's been a long time."

My face twists in disgust. His strip club 'habits' are the reason Mom left in the first place, although not without a nice chunk of his money. Dad used to conduct a lot of business there, schmoozing potential new clients and getting serviced.

The only reason I went there all those years ago was as a present from him for doing so well in school. Dad thought it would be a good way to start learning the ropes, and I idolized him then. I would have done anything to make him proud of me at the time.

He sent me there with a few friends whose family were part of other well-known companies. He wanted me to start the process of gaining new clientele and paid for the whole night—alcohol, private dances, and *her*. *Ember.* My recurrent wet dream. I saw her on stage and knew I had to have her. Was I a bastard for it?

Yes. I know I was.

"No, thanks. I'm sure if they won't give you an invitation, they have a reason. Later."

"Boy, you listen to me," he cuts in, his tone condescending, "I made you into what you are. Don't be an ungrateful bastard for it. If it wasn't for me stepping down, you'd still be—"

Oh, this is a laugh. "You didn't step down. The board *forced* you out," I grit through my clenched jaw. Anger pulses through my veins like fire, ready to disintegrate anything that comes close. "If I remember correctly, you caught some heat for your love of women and questionable morals. Thanks anyway, Dad. I always enjoy these pleasant chats with you. Go fuck yourself."

I end the call before I have to listen to anything else coming out of his mouth. Times like this I wish I was on a phone I could slam down. It was always so much more satisfying.

I search for the strip club online, but there isn't much that's easily accessible. The phone number and address are listed at the top, and there are a few small local articles from years ago talking about the new business and how applications were open for potential clients.

The last article I find is a *Forbes thirty under thirty* list. It's an article about the owners, a group of four women who go by The Madams, and it talks about their journey and why it was important for them to open a club run by women.

It's fascinating the way these women see the club. They see it as a safe haven, which is the complete opposite of how I think any man would ever see it. These women offer emotional support, along with self-defense and some of the most state-of-the-art technology to keep their workers safe.

According to the article, in order to become a member, each patron has to undergo an extensive background check. Only if everything clears are they allowed in. I never gave my permission for anyone to do a background check on me, especially not for a membership.

There must be someone who's able to give me some sort of information as to when I agreed to have my background looked into. I dial the number from the website, and it rings before switching over to voicemail.

"Hello, this is Ethan Freeman. I need some information about my membership status. Please call me back as soon as you can."

It's nine o'clock when my phone rings with a restricted number. "It's Ethan."

"Hello, Mr. Freeman. You called earlier inquiring about your membership status?" a sultry voice over on the other end asks.

"Yes. How long have I been a paying member of the club?"

"According to our records, you have been a member since we first opened eight years ago."

What? "I don't understand." I shake my head, trying to rack my brain. "I never gave my permission for a background check. According to what I've read, you don't allow members to join without it. I also have never received a bill."

"Yes. That's correct. However, according to what I see here, you know one of the girls who works here, and she signed you up under good faith."

My eyebrows shoot up to my hairline. "Who?"

"I'm sorry, I'm unable to give you that information," she replies coolly.

I tug on my hair in frustration. "What do you mean, you can't give me that information?"

"You're in good standing here at *RISE*. Why not come by and see if you can locate your friend? Is there anything else I can do for you this evening?"

"No," I growl, then think better of it. "Actually, does Ember work there?"

"Madam Ember is here, yes. She'll be on the main stage soon."

"I'm on my way. I want a private show with her." I hang up before she can respond and rush to my car.

If I can't fuck Addison, hopefully, I can get the next best thing. The traffic is light into the city, and I pull into the full parking lot in only a few minutes. All the cars in the lot are nice and expensive. I wouldn't expect anything less when the dues every year are five-thousand. There's not a line outside, so I give the bouncer my name.

He ushers me inside where a woman greets me and shows me to a table. I ask the girl if Ember has been on stage yet, and when she tells me she's up next, my heart pounds against my chest.

I feel like a twenty-two-year-old all over again. It's exciting, almost forbidden. A smile spreads across my face as the lights go down and the last girl exits the stage, shrugging back into her clothes. The steady bass drum of the song starts, and the DJ announces Madam Ember to the stage. Random whistles and hoots can be heard around the room, and I sink lower into my seat to watch.

I'm not sure why, but I feel like I'm in trouble, like I shouldn't be here watching her dance. It's almost like someone is going to pop up from the shadows and tell me I've been caught with my hand down my pants. Not that my hand is anywhere near my pants, for the record. Not yet anyway.

The lights come up and her back is to the audience, her long red hair flowing down her back and her toned legs on full display. She glances over her shoulder, and I swear she looks right at me and winks from behind a bright pink mask before she starts a slow turn around the pole, sliding her hands up and down it as if it were something else.

I motion for one of the girls to come over. She bends down

to hear me over the music, and without breaking eye contact, I say, "I want a private show with her."

"I'll put in your request, and if she accepts, someone will be by shortly to get you."

I haven't been laid in months, and she might just take the edge off.

CHAPTER 5

ADDISON

I *can't believe Ethan is here watching my show.* When Eden said he'd called today and was snooping around, I did a little happy dance until I saw the fear in her eyes. She knows the type of man he is. I've told her one too many times. He's looking for information about his membership. I knew he was going to; I just didn't think it would happen so fast.

And Ethan will stop at nothing until he gets answers.

I need to make sure that doesn't happen. The music is blaring from the speakers next to the stage, and I'm doing my pole routine on auto-pilot as I watch Ethan enjoying my show. I roll my hips along the pole, and I swear my insides are turning to a puddle of goo. He's not doing anything out of the ordinary, drinking out of the tumbler in his hand, but I see the fire in his eyes, even from this distance.

I crawl to the edge of the stage to get as close to him as I can, then blow him a kiss and a wink before turning to sit on my butt and push myself back. He bites his lip and soothes it with his tongue. God, the look he's giving me shoots straight to my core, and I know if I can't find some relief soon, I'm going to be in trouble.

I usually like staying on stage for as long as I can, but tonight, I can't wait to leave. I'm hoping to entice him to a room. Maybe I can show him how much better my skills have gotten. How much I've learned since we were together eight years ago. *Maybe he's learned some new tricks, too.*

The song ends with me on my knees, my head bowed, and my bra somewhere next to me. Bills are being thrown at me, but I don't care about that. I usually give my dancing tips to some of the other girls, or ones that are in need of it. Between owning *RISE* and working at *Emulation*, I do just fine. I try to peak out at Ethan from behind my mask, but he's no longer at the table. My heart drops to my stomach, and I stand on shaky legs as the lights go down to leave the stage.

Candy said he wanted a private dance tonight, didn't she? I frown as I leave the stage.

As soon as I step backstage, Eden is waiting for me. Her arms are crossed over her chest, and her Madam Roxie persona is locked tightly in place.

"Ethan wants a show."

I try to hide my smile because I know she's not happy with me right now. "He wasn't there, though, at the end of the set," I say, confused.

"I already brought him back to your room." She reaches out for me and grasps my forearm. "He can't know, Addy," Eden says, stepping into the dim light.

I know what she's talking about, and I nod in agreement. "I'll figure it out."

I all but run to my room, *Madam Ember's Lair*, and stop directly outside, catching my breath. I look at my clothes and fix my short skirt in place, then straighten out my thigh highs.

I reach for the metal knob and turn it, my breathing returning to normal, but my heart is racing and my mouth is dry. *I shouldn't have rushed to get to him.* I push open the door, and he's standing in the middle of the room. He turns and smirks as he hears the door open.

"Hello, Ember," he says, and it makes my heart skip a beat. His voice is husky as his eyes trace every curve of my body. *I'd love to hear him call me Addison, my real name, in that tone.* How is it possible one man can make me soaked by only saying two little words?

"Hello, Ethan." I close the door behind me, and even though my body is screaming at me to move closer, I stay where I am, watching him. Damn does he look good. He's in a pair of dress slacks and a black button-down top. My tongue peeks out to lick my lips. He mirrors my action, and the two of us stand there frozen, staring, until I finally find my voice again. "I haven't seen you in a long time. What brought you here?"

He takes a step closer, pulls a sip from his drink, and places it on the small table next to him, the ice clinking against the glass. "I didn't think you'd still be at a place like this after all these years. The red hair suits you." He motions toward the mask covering the top half of my face. "Can you take that off? It's a bit distracting."

"No. It stays on."

His eyes darken, but this is Ethan Freeman, my boss. I know he would never hurt me, but with the look he's giving Ember right now, I'm not so sure about her. "You requested a private show. What can I do for you? Would you like me to dance?"

"Do you want to dance?" His words ring around me, and I'm transported back to being a nineteen-year-old girl again. Those are the same words he spoke to me before he had me pressed against a wall, fingering me until I came. I gasp but refuse to move. "Why are you paying for my membership, Ember?"

How the fuck has he figured it out so fast? "I-I don't know what you're talking about." *Shit. This is bad.* The one thing Ethan hates is liars, and he must be able to read me like a book. My palms are sweaty, I'm struggling to breathe normally. He has me so frazzled I'm starting to stutter.

"Well, the only time I was in a strip club is when my father paid for a night at *The Devil's Playground*, and I had sex with you." He takes another step closer. The lion is closing in on his prey. "Then, the place burned down, a new strip club—"

"Gentleman's club," I correct him.

He smiles and my heart does a flip. He doesn't smile that often anymore. Too consumed with work. "Gentleman's club opens, and it turns out it is owned by a group of women, one of which happens to be the woman I slept with almost ten years ago. I've asked, and no one knows who's been paying my dues. It's not coming out of my company's account, and I haven't received any bills. So, that leaves you." He reaches out and rubs the ends of my red wig between his thumb and forefinger before dropping it.

He's so close I can smell his cologne, and I want to melt. It's the same scent he wears to the office, and it's a distraction. When I smell it first thing in the morning, I breathe deep, filling my senses with it until I can't smell it anymore. If not, I'll never get through my day.

"Ethan," I say breathlessly. His eyes darken as he inhales deeply, his nostrils flaring. He takes another small step closer, and now I can feel the heat coming from his body. I reach my hand out, placing it on his chest. His heart beats in a steady rhythm, which helps to calm my racing nerves.

"I like how you say my name. Say it again," he requests, placing his large hand over mine, holding me to him. It may be a request, but I know how commanding he is, and that's how I take it.

"Ethan." I swallow past the lump forming in my throat and look down at our feet. "I'm not paying your dues. If you were lucky enough to be put on the member list, you should be thankful. A lot of people have been trying to get a membership, and we won't allow them in." I pull my hand loose from his and skirt around him, giving myself some room to breathe.

He snorts. "I know. My father asked me to get him in."

I spin to face him, my hair falling over my shoulders. "No. He's banned from this place." My skin crawls thinking of all the times he asked for a private show from me. Vince used to spend a lot of time talking with Paul Freeman. I never knew what about, but if they were chummy, it was for nothing good.

There was only one time I caved to give him what he wanted, but I refused to sleep with him. I would give him a dance but that's it. I knew who he was, and I thought he would be like his son. Let me tell you, that apple fell *very* far from the tree. Paul is an asshole and abuser.

When I told him I couldn't sleep with him, he slapped me across the face and tried to force it. If it weren't for the roofie I slipped into his drink without him knowing, it could have ended very badly. He stumbled out of the room, calling me a whore and a filthy slut.

He didn't even pay for the dance, which meant I had to pay Vince back for the time lost by me 'not doing my job properly.' I don't even know what that payment would have looked like. Eden took care of him for the night, not allowing me to deal with the aftermath of losing a 'top customer,' as Vince called him.

"Duly noted. I don't have much to do with him anyway, so that won't be a problem." I turn my back to him, and he moves behind me. He places his hand on my shoulders and kisses my neck, next to my tattoo. He then traces his finger over the design, which is illuminated because of the black lights in the room. "I like your tattoo." He takes a deep breath. "Why do I feel like I know you?"

I can't go through with it. I've put this man up on a pedestal for so long that it doesn't seem real. I turn in his embrace and look into his eyes. "I'll give you a dance, but I won't sleep with you tonight, Ethan. If you don't like it, then you can leave. I won't think anything of it." I slide my hand between us to feel how hard he is.

Jesus, he's just as big as I remember, and he's hard as a rock for me. I pull in a shaky breath, and he pulls my hand off him gently before placing a kiss right next to my lips.

"I'll see myself out." He turns on his heel and leaves without another word. The walls seem like they're closing in on me. That was too close. *What if he's not like how I remember him?* In my mind, Ethan is a god, has been ever since the first time I met him. Why the hell couldn't I just sleep with him, get it out of my system?

A knock sounds at the door a few minutes later, and I tell the person to enter. It's Eden.

"Don't say anything," I say, annoyed.

"I wasn't going to. Do you want to talk about it?" She stands next to me and rubs my arm in comfort.

"No. You were right; he's snooping for information. He asked if I've been paying his dues. I lied, but it's a matter of time before he puts two and two together." I sigh and push my mask up over my face. "I'll handle it. I won't put you, the other girls, or this place at risk."

She pulls me in for a hug. "Go home, Addy."

I nod and leave her standing there to go collect my stuff. I toss on my t-shirt and jeans, hang up my wig, and leave through the back door. The club will be open for another few hours, but the other girls can take care of it. I want to go lie down and figure out how I'm going to fix the potential mess I've created.

There has to be a way I can get it on the books at the company, or somehow give him the information without getting caught. I'll figure it out. I just need a bit of time to do it.

———

MONDAY MORNING AND I STILL HAVEN'T FIGURED OUT A DAMN thing. I email Bill in accounting first thing to see if Ethan has reached out to him. The only plan I have is to try to convince him to tell Ethan there is something on the books. When I arrive, though, he's already in Ethan's office.

Shit.

Bill comes out of his office a few minutes later and nods in my direction.

"Bill, is everything okay?" I ask.

"Yeah, he's just looking into a few things. I told him I'd have some answers for him this afternoon."

"Is it about the membership?"

He stops mid-step and turns to look at me, his mouth turned down in a frown. "What membership?"

I resist the urge to drop my face into my hands and shake my head. Could this get any worse? I'm going to give myself away without even realizing it. "Never mind. He had asked me a question this weekend, but I didn't have an answer for him. I assumed he was asking you about it."

"No, he was asking me to run some numbers in regards to

purchasing a company. Wanted to find out what kind of budget he's working with."

"Ms. Snyder," Ethan calls from the doorway and beckons me with his finger. "A word, please?"

I stand, smooth out my skirt, and enter the lion's den.

CHAPTER 6

ETHAN

I've been going crazy since this weekend between not getting any, trying to unravel the mystery about my dues, and the conversation with my dad. I thought Ember would have helped with one of my problems, possibly two, but instead, she sent me on my way. And there was something so damn familiar about her. I can't put my finger on it, but it's like I've been in her presence lately.

Addison sashays into my office, the skirt moving around her hips. My eyes crawl over her form—her shapely legs, petite waist, and perfect breasts. Everything about this woman drives me crazy. She stands at the ready, her tablet in hand. Such a good worker. *My good girl.* Every time I'm in the room with her alone, my mind wanders.

I was able to keep my thoughts at bay for so long, but the longer I work with her, the more I want to be inside her. I want to fuck my assistant, and there's not a damn thing I can do about it. Unless I move her out of the position.

"Do you like being my assistant?"

She blinks at me twice, not expecting the question, and

takes a deep breath. "It's challenging at times, but yes. I enjoy the job."

"Why?" I cross my arms over my chest, waiting for her response.

She shrugs, but I see the confusion all over her face. Her eyebrows are drawn tight, and her perfect lips are turned down in a frown. "It's busy. Your calendar is a lot to handle, but I like to prove I can do anything. I like to prove it to myself, as well as to you."

My lips twitch in a smirk. "Good girl," I whisper.

She lowers her eyes, and a blush covers her cheeks and neck. "Thank you... Sir." She whispers the last word. I stalk over to her, encroaching on her space. She takes a small step back from me, and I grab her wrist, holding her in place.

I lean down, my lips pressed against her ear, and whisper, "Do you have any idea what you do to me?" I've been watching her for some time, even though she doesn't have a clue. When I'm close, her breathing changes. And not because she's scared of me, either. She wants me. I know she does. I just have to find a way to get her to act upon her desires.

She turns her head a fraction, my lips now almost against her cheek. "What do I do to you?" Her words are breathless, and I can almost hear her heart banging against her ribs.

"You turn me on so fucking much, I want to bend you over my desk, lift your skirt, and fuck you senseless." I take her hand and place it over my throbbing cock, letting her feel exactly what she does to me.

She whimpers and bites her lip. "Why haven't you then, Sir?"

She clears her throat. "Mr. Freeman? Are you okay?"

I blink and shake the thoughts from my head. "What? Shit. I'm sorry, Addy. I didn't get a lot of sleep this weekend. I must be more tired than I thought." *Great, now my daydreams are feeling too fucking real.*

"Want me to run to the coffee shop next door and get you something?" She hugs the tablet to her chest and smiles brightly at me.

"Sure. That would be great. When you get back, we can talk about the meeting with Mr. Hughes. Have you gotten it set up yet?"

She nods. "Yes. His secretary got back to me a few minutes ago. You have a meeting set up for Wednesday."

This is too easy. Patrick is going to be eating out of the palm of my hand before long. I'll get the usual team together, and it shouldn't be hard to win this one over. I'm sure he's already pissing his pants just thinking about the cracks in his system. Not that it was hard for my guys to break in. He really needs to hire a company with strong security ties if he doesn't want his personal business out there.

She turns and walks out, and that's when I notice something on her lower neck. It blends in with her skin, almost like a scar or something. I wonder what the story is there. She usually wears her hair down, but today it is pulled up and away from her neck.

When she gets back, we need to go over the events for the ball this weekend and what I expect of her. I usually call a girl from my little black book, but I need someone that will actually be able to help me. The board has been riding my ass about bringing on a few larger clients, and Penn Sandolval is the one I'm after at the charity ball.

If I give Addison his name, she can get me all sorts of information on him, and I can use it to my advantage. I can also get her a list of people who are going to be there; I know she'll help keep them straight for me. I get to kill two birds with one stone—a pretty girl on my arm, and she will help me win over the clients.

Thoughts of Madam Ember infiltrate my mind. I'm still

trying to find more information on the owners of *RISE*. I haven't been able to break into their systems. They must have hired a good company to keep their records safe. All I've been able to get is the holding company's name. *Johnson and Smith Associates.* So, of course, they were my next search, and all I got is it's an attorney's office. Big shocker there.

Addison steps back into my office with coffees in hand and sits, waiting for me to give her instructions.

"The ball this weekend, it's a masquerade. Find an appropriate dress and mask, and you can expense it to the company since you'll be working. Black tie."

"Okay, and what will I be doing for the evening, Mr. Freeman?"

"Be my date and help me keep the names of some beneficiaries straight, along with having information ready on Penn Sandolval."

Her eyes shoot up to her hairline. "Y-your date?"

"Yes. I need you there to help me, and I need a date. Kill two birds with one stone." She still doesn't seem appeased with my answer, but she hasn't shot me down yet either. "I'll make sure to work a nice bonus into your pay."

She rolls her eyes but nods. "Okay. Well, I need to go shopping then. Is there a certain color I should get?"

"I'm sure whatever you pick will be fine. I'll be by to pick you up at six sharp. Be ready."

She huffs and leaves my office without another word. Despite me telling her this is simply for work, I'm excited to have her as my date. Most of the women I bring to things like this are just looking to see how deep my pockets go. I learned a long time to not trust any of those women. Addy is safe. She'll be a good date for the evening.

As long as I don't take her home to my bed.

THE MEETING WITH PATRICK HUGHES HAS GONE EXACTLY TO plan. He was happy I contacted his office due to some system discrepancies his teams have uncovered. I had to work hard to suppress my smile, knowing I'm the mastermind behind those issues. I've been doing this long enough that I've learned to keep a good poker face.

By the time I return to the office, Addison has already received the go-ahead from Patrick to draw up a proposal on how we will cover his security from here on out. *It's like taking candy from a baby.* I knew it would be easy, but I didn't think it would be *that* easy.

She hands me my messages without saying a word, and I look over them as I drop my stuff off in the office. One is from my old friend from high school, Callan Manning. We played ball together back in the day. Last I heard, he's been jet setting around the world. I wonder why he didn't call my cell.

"Hey, man, long time no talk. Too good for your old friends now that you're Mister Big Shot CEO?" Cal teases as he answers.

"I could say the same thing about you, the hotshot book model. Bet all the women are throwing themselves at your feet, hoping to be taken by the rogue pirate," I snicker.

"Very funny. Never heard that one before. At least I'm getting laid by horny women. When's the last time you've fucked something other than your hand?" he badgers; he never takes anything seriously.

I rub my forehead. I'm not going to dignify that question with an answer, but it has been a while. I thought for sure I'd be sleeping with Ember this weekend, but she blew me off. Nothing kills a hard-on faster than a disinterested girl.

"What do you want?" I grumble, my mood deteriorating at the thought of Ember's rejection.

"I gotta go to this stupid charity ball thing and saw your name on the roster of attendees. Thought we could hang. Thing is, all the chicks my sister has tried to set me up with lately have me pegged as some freakin' Dom like in that smut shit they all read. Don't get me wrong, it was fun to start with, but I'm over it. I thought maybe you had someone I could take out on a date, no strings attached."

"Since when do you need help getting a date, Cal?" I roll my eyes.

He sighs. "Well, you have one, I assume?"

"Yes," I draw out the S.

"Then ask your date to bring a girlfriend for me. Easy peasy."

I shake my head and look toward the closed door of my office, imagining Addison sitting at her desk, typing away. "My date isn't really a traditional one in the sense. She's my assistant. We are going together strictly for business."

"Dude, are you banging your assistant? I thought your dad taught you better than that." He gives a hearty laugh.

"Fuck you, Cal," I say through clenched teeth, my mood worsening.

"Calm down, tiger." He sighs. "Look, ask her to ask a friend. If she says no, I'll figure something out, but at least ask."

"Fine." I hang up as fast as I can, not wanting to hear another word from his arrogant mouth. He knows comparing me to my father is the biggest insult he can muster. I take a few deep breaths and open the door. Addy looks up at me, waiting.

Images of her on her knees in front of me flash through my mind before I can stop them.

"Can I help you, Mr. Freeman?" she asks, her voice like sin.

I clear my throat. "I just got off the phone with Cal

Manning. He's also going to be attending the ball this weekend, and he needs a date. I told him I would ask if you have any friends to go with him."

Her lips pull up into a smile. "Is he not able to get his own date?"

I rub the back of my neck. "It's..." I roll my eyes again, his cockiness annoying to me all of a sudden. "It's complicated. I mean, if you have a friend you can set him up with, fine. If not, it's no big deal. He doesn't want to go with another girl that his sister sets him up with. I told him I would at least ask you."

Her smile widens. "I actually have the perfect girl in mind. I have a friend who needs to get out there a bit more, and she's very pretty." She unlocks her phone and shows me a picture of her and the girl. She's pretty and tall. I'm sure she'll give Cal a run for his money.

"Perfect. Make sure she has something appropriate to wear, and don't forget the masks."

"Of course. The mask is crucial." She smiles at me, and I turn on my heel back to my office. I close the door behind me and walk into my private bathroom. My dick is hard as a rock, and I'm surprised Addy didn't notice it, although I did discreetly try to hide it from her view. *Get a hold of yourself, Ethan.*

I glance down at my bulge, look at the closed door, and make up my mind. Fuck it. I need to do something about this before I embarrass myself further. I grab a towel from the counter, unzip my pants, and go to work.

CHAPTER 7

ADDISON

"Please, Eden? You can be Roxie for the night if you want to be. You don't have to tell him your real name, and you're going to be wearing a mask. Please do this for me?" I beg. I don't like to let Ethan down, and if Eden doesn't accept, I don't have a back-up plan. Lia and Everleigh are both married with kids. I don't have any other close girlfriends that I could ask, and I'm not asking one of the girls from the club.

She sighs. "I—I don't have a dress."

I shake my fists in excitement. I knew I could convince her to come. "Thank you. I promise I'll make this up to you. We'll go shopping tonight."

"So, who's my date for this thing?"

"Cal Manning."

"What?" she yells into the phone. I pull it away from my ear and wince at the volume. "Oh, no. There's *no* way I can go with him."

"Why not? You can't tell me yes and then take it back. Unwritten rule of friendship."

"Do you even know who he *is*?" she asks, her voice still a bit high.

"Um... no. Should I?"

"He's a big shot book model, and I absolutely swoon over him. He's gorgeous... and dreamy... and so fucking hot."

"Well, if you're Roxie, you don't have to worry about him knowing who you are..." I coax.

The line is silent for a beat, and I know she's going to say yes. She doesn't have a good excuse as to why she can't come. She's not working that night. "You're buying my dress."

"I love you, Eady. Thank you. Ethan is going to get us at six Saturday night. Come to my apartment and we'll get ready together."

I jump out of my seat with a huge smile on my face, excited to tell Ethan that Callan has a date. I smooth my skirt and stand in front of Ethan's office door. I knock and push it open without waiting for his reply. He's in the bathroom with the door closed. I take a seat and wait for him to finish so I can tell him right away and he can cross one thing off his extensive list.

I hear him grunt behind the door and then breathe a heavy sigh in relief. *Oh my God! He's jacking off in there.* My face heats up as I picture his large hands over his equally large cock. Picturing him sliding his hand up and down. My hand slides between my legs, and I rub over my engorged clit a few times before I mentally slap myself.

Not professional, Addy!

I pull my hand away and fix my skirt. *Jesus, I wish I could watch him.* I wonder who he's thinking of. Too many thoughts are running around in my mind, and I now know I shouldn't be here. I stand, and just as I reach for the door handle, I hear him behind me.

"Addy, what are you doing in here?" His voice is tight. He

looks back at the open bathroom door, and I peek past him to see a towel on the edge of the sink.

"I-ah… I knocked. I wanted to tell you my friend agreed to be Cal's date for Saturday."

"How long have you been here?" he asks, his eyes narrowing, daring me to lie to him.

"Only about a minute. I thought you were just using the restroom," I squeak and lower my chin. I can't look at him. If I do, I know my own feelings and desires will reflect back. How badly I want it to be me he thinks of when playing with himself. How badly I want to be the one to bring him pleasure.

"What's your friend's name? I'll let Callan know, and the four of us will go together."

I'm thankful that he's decided to ignore this little incident for now. "Uh, Ro-Roxanne. I'll make sure she gets ready over at my place."

"Great." I peer up at him, waiting for… I don't know what. His jaw is locked as he crosses his arms over his chest. "Anything else?"

"N-no, Mr. Freeman." I slink out of his office and close the door behind me. Normally, he wouldn't intimidate me, but today, today is different. I'm too turned on to fight back. I can't look at him any longer without wanting to jump his bones. I need to get out of here. I type up a quick email telling him I'm going to an early lunch and gather my stuff.

I walk the few blocks to *Johnson and Smith Associates* and pull open the door. The robust woman behind the desk smiles warmly at me. "Hi, Addison. What can I do for you today?"

"Hi, Linda, is Maxwell in? I need to speak to him."

Before she can respond, he comes into view. "Ms. Snyder, to what do I owe the pleasure?"

"We need to talk. It's important." He jerks his head for me to follow him, and I take a seat in his office as he closes the door. "I pay for a member's dues, but he doesn't know it's me. He's now been snooping around to find out who pays them, and I know he'll be reaching out to you. Our files are locked tight, but I know he's snooping."

"This wouldn't be Ethan Freeman, would it?" I pull my bottom lip between my teeth and nod, my eyes wide with worry. "It's your business, so I won't question it. He left a message for me, but I haven't called him back yet. I was going to call Ms. Riser to ask about it."

"I need him to stop snooping, and I thought I would be able to fudge a few things to make it look like it was coming from his company, but he got in touch with accounting before I could." I drop my head into my hands. "I don't know what to do."

"I believe he did a small project for our firm years back. I'll call him back and come up with a story. I'll tell him we offered him a membership for work he did, free of charge or something. I'll handle it."

I take a deep breath and look at him, relief washing over me. I give him a warm smile. "Thank you, Maxwell. I don't know what we would do without you."

He smirks and nods his head in understanding. "I'll keep you posted, but don't worry about it."

I walk out feeling better than I have in days and stop to get another coffee for Ethan and me. When I step into his office, he's seething. His hands are clenched by his sides and his face is red. He takes one look at me, and his features soften before three long strides put him directly in front of me. Reaching his hands out to put them on my shoulders, he then drops them at the last minute.

"I know you heard more than you're telling me, and I want to apologize. It was very unprofessional of me, and I promise it won't happen again. I would prefer if you didn't go to HR with this, but I understand if you feel you must." He takes the coffee from my outstretched hand as I try to come up with what to say.

"Ethan," he snaps his head up to look at me, and I can't decipher the look he gives me. Maybe it's lust, want, temptation? *If only.* "This is your office, and I shouldn't have walked in. I'll make sure to wait next time. It'll be our secret."

He furrows his brows, and his mouth is popped open in disbelief. I know what he's probably thinking. Most women would jump at the chance to tell this juicy story, but I would never do anything to hurt him like that, even if he doesn't know it.

"You're something else, has anyone ever told you that?"

I feel my face heat up, and I look to the ground. *You did once, a long time ago.* "Not in recent years."

"Well, your boyfriend is an idiot for not saying it more often."

"What boyfriend?" I look up at him from under my lashes, and he stops mid-sip and watches me. *Why the fuck did I say that? God, could I sound any needier?* "Listen, I'm going to take off early so Roxanne and I can find some dresses for this weekend. If you need anything, let me know. I'll see you tomorrow, Mr. Freeman." The words rush past my lips, and I'm out the door before he can find his voice again.

CHAPTER 8

ETHAN

"Remember, Cal, Addison is my assistant, and Roxanne is her friend. Don't be an ass and make me look bad. I went out on a limb to get you this date."

"Yeah, yeah, I get it. Don't sleep with her," he says as he rolls his eyes.

It may have been the tenth time since I got him the date that I've lectured him. The last thing I need after the bathroom incident this week is for her friend to somehow get hurt because I made Addy set up the date. I haven't been able to get what she said out of my head.

What boyfriend?

I thought for sure she had some lucky asshole in her life. Honestly, if she did have someone in her life, it would make it easier for me to behave. Instead, the beast within wants to be unleashed on her. It's getting harder and harder to keep him chained and locked away.

The limo rolls up in front of a nice apartment complex, and we get out. *Damn, maybe I'm paying her too much if she can afford a place like this.*

"Damn, nice place," Cal says.

The doorman lets us into the building, and we take the elevator to the fifth floor. When the doors open, there are only two doors on the floor. I knock on apartment five-zero-one, and Addy opens the door with a smile on her face. "Ethan," she gasps and clears her throat. "Hi, come on in. I just need to get my bag and we can be on our way."

She stuffs some note cards in her purse and walks down the hall. She's in a floor-length red dress with a V-neck neckline that plunges, stopping mid-back. Her hair is pulled up in a loose bun with some curls cascading down. She's a knockout. I couldn't have a prettier girl on my arm even if I tried.

She comes back a moment later with her friend in tow. She is wearing an equally dazzling dress in black, with a lace bodice and sweetheart neckline.

"Mr. Freeman, Mr. Manning, this is my good friend Rox—" she introduces.

"Roxanne." The friend steps forward, interrupting Addison and glaring at her even as Addy frowns.

Cal takes a step forward, hand outstretched to take hers in his. "It's a pleasure to meet you, Roxanne. I'm Callan Manning, but you can call me Cal. I can say without a doubt, I will have the prettiest girl on my arm tonight." He flashes a megawatt smile at her.

She giggles. *Giggles!* "Nice to meet you, Cal."

As the two of them are involved in their own little conversation, I stand next to Addy and place my hands on her upper arms, then lean down so my lips are by her ear. I can't keep myself from touching her any longer, and since she is my date for the night, I have an excuse. "What are the notecards you placed in your purse?"

"I requested a list of everyone who will be there and have been reviewing the names and their occupations. I managed to find some of their pictures online, so they're included as well."

I can't help but smile. "You really are something else. I need one more favor tonight."

"What's that?" She turns to face me, and I have to pull back, her lips only centimeters from mine. I smell her minty breath as it fans across my face.

"Call me Ethan."

She smirks. "I'm working tonight, and you're my boss."

"Yes, but you also told me you wouldn't call me Ethan when in the office. We won't be in the office tonight."

She blushes and tries my name on her tongue. "Okay, Ethan."

Instant hard-on. *Fuck.* Maybe this was a bad idea. I'm about to open my stupid mouth again when Cal insists we get going so we're not late. He takes Roxanne's arm and slides it through his, but when I try to take Addy's, she moves out of my grasp.

Maybe not...

The ride feels too long, especially with her so close to me. When we arrive, we slide our masks into place, and I get the feeling of déjà vu. I've seen her mask before, or I *think* I have. It's light pink with silver along the edges and a few jewels under the eye holes. I slide out first, and she allows me to help her, even wrap my arm around her waist. At her apartment, she didn't have to play the game, but here, she knows she has to.

She puts on a large smile, and the entire place lights up. Cal and I leave the ladies to go to the bar for some drinks. No way I'll get through this night without some alcohol. These things are always so boring, but it's a great way to network and talk business. Alcohol makes people more receptive to talk about deals. Tickets are expensive, so if you're seen here, you have to be someone important.

"Roxanne and Addison are fucking knockouts. You sure you aren't banging your assistant?" Cal asks as the bartender hands us our drinks.

"If only," I murmur. "I'd give my left nut to be able to take her on a real date. That's why I asked her to come with me, under the guise of needing her help tonight. Truth be told, that part will be helpful, but I really wanted to spend the night with her and not have to worry about some gold digger."

The ladies come into view, and we hand over drinks. Cal and Roxanne step away from us as Addy looks anywhere but at me. She starts pointing out some of the attendees and what companies they work for. I take a sip of my drink and watch as she does what she does best, feigning interest in the people she's pointing out.

"Do you want to dance?" I cut in.

She stops mid-sentence and looks up at me. "But no one's dancing."

I shrug. "So? Who says we can't be the talk of the town?"

I take her glass from her, depositing it on a nearby table, then reach my hand out for hers. Her delicate fingers slide into my palm, and I escort her to the dance floor. I wrap my left arm around her lower back and keep her right hand in mine as we slowly start to sway to the music. She doesn't even fight me as I take the lead.

"I didn't know you could dance, Mr. Freeman."

"Ethan. And yeah, my mom made me take lessons when I was little. She told me when I got older, I could get any girl I wanted if I could dance. She was right. All the girls at the dances wanted to go with me once they learned I knew how. You're not so bad yourself. When did you learn?"

"About ten years ago. I have some pretty great friends who showed me how."

"I'll have to meet these friends of yours sometime."

She feels so good in my embrace and fits in my arms like she's meant to be there. I've never met anyone like her before. She surprises me at every turn, and that's no easy feat, especially in my position.

The music changes, and a few people clap as we leave the dance floor. She blushes behind her mask as we walk to the bar and order another drink. She takes the glass of champagne from the bartender and gulps it down, ordering another one.

"Ethan, great to see you again," a man says behind us. I turn to see Al Costanza, CFO of Black Tie Rentals, walking toward us. I've tried to stay as far from this man as possible. He came to me a few years ago, asking about setting up some system securities for the company, and I politely declined, much to the board's disappointment. There are too many rumors flying around that I don't want anything to do with.

Addy takes a deep breath before speaking. "That's Al Costanza—"

I give her hand a gentle squeeze, letting her know I don't need her help with this one, and she closes her mouth and drinks the next glass of champagne.

"Mr. Costanza, nice to see you again." I reach my hand out to shake his.

"And who is this beautiful woman on your arm tonight?"

"My date. Ashley," I lie, as I place my hand on the small of her back. She looks at me, questioning my name choice before she faces him, a beautiful smile plastered to her face.

"Nice to meet you, sir." She places the flute to her lips to take a generous sip, his eyes never leaving her. "Excuse me, gentlemen. I need to use the ladies' room." She finishes her drink and places it on the bar.

She walks off in the direction that Roxanne and Cal are. Addy links arms with Roxanne, and the two ladies head toward the door.

"Beautiful date you have on your arm tonight." I give him a courteous nod. "So, I have a job I need some help with, and I thought you might be interested. Do you have a few minutes to talk?" He's saying the words to me, but he's looking in the direction of Addy and Roxanne.

"I actually need to track down Penn Sandolval, if you'll excuse me."

"He couldn't make it tonight, but we've been business partners for years, I know what type of services he's looking for. Let's chat."

I sigh, left with no other options, and agree to the damn conversation.

CHAPTER 9

ADDISON

"Eady, ladies' room, now," I whisper into Eden's ear, giving Cal a warm smile.

"Excuse us, Cal. We need to use the ladies' room. I'll be right back," Eden says to Cal with a little grin.

We calmly walk to the ladies' room, but my stomach is doing flips. *Is Ethan ashamed of me?*

We check the stalls, and when I know the coast is clear, she locks the door. She pulls her mask off and watches me, waiting for me to tell her why I'm in a panic.

"Ethan just told someone I was his date, *Ashley*. Why the hell would he do that?"

She cocks her perfectly sculpted eyebrow at me. "That does seem odd. He must have a good reason for it. Did you try asking him?" Logical answer. Not what I wanted her to say, but it's just like her to give common sense advice.

"No, he was talking with someone about business, and I excused myself to talk to you. Doesn't that seem odd, though?"

She shrugs. "I don't know what to tell you."

A knock on the door makes both of us jump. I place my hand over my heart as Eden smirks at me. I swear, nothing scares this girl. "Ladies, is everything okay in here?" Ethan's muffled voice floats through the door.

I let out a slow breath and close my eyes. "Be out in a minute." We both fix our masks before I unlock the door, putting a big smile on my face.

"Dinner is going to be served in a minute." He hands me another glass of champagne and escorts both of us to the table like the perfect gentleman he is.

I'm lost in my thoughts. I push around a green bean and roasted potato as I try to seem interested, listening to the speaker drone on about something boring. I know I need to eat something—the glasses of champagne are starting to do a number on me—but I can't. Eden has nudged me too many times to count, and now Ethan is looking at me strangely.

"Hey, you okay? You've hardly touched your food," he says softly.

Just ask him about the name, chicken shit! "Yeah, just not very hungry," I take another sip of my champagne and smile. Al, the man Ethan was talking to, seems to have disappeared. The waitress places a slice of cheesecake in front of me, and my mouth waters. I grab my fork and dig in, trying not to drop crumbs on myself. Ethan chuckles, and when I look at him, he shakes his head.

"Thought you weren't hungry?"

I blush. "Okay, maybe I am, a little." He puts his dessert plate in front of me and winks. This man knows the way to my heart. If it's not with a cock between my legs, it's with desserts!

Ethan finishes a conversation just as the lights dim and the music changes to a livelier beat. Cal helps Eden stand, and the two of them make their way to the dance floor. I turn my head to watch them. She looks so happy wrapped in his arms, like she's meant to be there. *I wish she would have told him her real name.* I know Eden has been down since Everleigh tied the knot. She deserves to find her happily ever after, too.

Ethan's finger draws over my tattoo on my neck, and I tense under his touch. "What's the scar from?"

I finish the glass in my hand and turn to face him, my vision blurring around the edges. "It's a tattoo. I got it a long time ago with some friends. We all have matching ones."

"What is it?"

"It's a secret." I put my finger to my lips and smirk behind it as if I'm telling him some inside joke. After *The Devil's Playground* was destroyed, the four of us got phoenix tattoos to symbolize our rebirth. It's a black-light tattoo, and in normal light, it almost resembles a scar. I place my hand on his thigh and give him a gentle squeeze. *It would be so easy to slide my hand up higher.* "Want to dance?"

He extends his hand, and I slide mine into his. Warmth radiates through my palm and down to the pit of my stomach where it settles and spreads. He turns me to face him and pulls me into his embrace as a slow song starts. I step in closer, our bodies so close they are practically touching everywhere.

His thumb brushes over the scar on my left wrist, and I fight to not pull back from him out of instinct. The memories of that day have mostly disappeared with time. I don't have nightmares like I used to, and I don't have to take pills to sleep, except around the anniversary of my family's death. I can't shake that date no matter how much I try. Normally, I pick up a shift at *RISE* to get my mind off things, sometimes sleep with someone. If I'm lucky, they are enough of a sadist that I feel numb the rest of the night.

"Why did you call me Ashley?" I ask, the burning question finally leaving my lips.

He's quiet for a minute, the music floating through the speakers drowning out everything around us. "There are rumors about Al Costanza, and I thought it was safer if he didn't know who I associate with."

"He's the CFO of one of the biggest rental companies in Atlanta. How bad can the man actually be? It could be great exposure for the company to align yourself with him," I offer, slipping into my assistant role with ease.

"Al and I have a history. He asked me to work on a project for him a few years back, and I had to decline. He's looking to use my company again. I told him to send me an email with what he needs and I'll take a look at it." His grip tightens on my lower back, and he pulls me even closer to him. My nose is basically nuzzled in the crook of his neck, and I can't help but take a deep breath.

"So, you're not ashamed that you're here with your assistant?" I ask, my voice sounding far off.

He pushes me out to look down into my eyes. "Why the hell would you think that?"

I shake my head. "It's the champagne talking. Don't mind me." I rest my cheek on his chest and inhale my favorite scent again—Ethan. His heart beats in a steady rhythm, and I don't even notice the song has changed until he tips his finger under my chin to make me look up at him.

"Want to go for a walk?"

I nod as he leads me off the dance floor. Eden and Cal are still tearing it up, and she's laughing—actually laughing. I don't get to see her that happy often, so it warms my heart. *You go, girl!* Ethan takes my hand, and we walk down a secluded hallway until we get to another empty room. I want him so bad. It would be so easy to lift my head, press my lips to his, and kiss him.

Would his lips be as soft as I remember them? Would the kiss be as good? I pull my bottom lip between my teeth and bite—hard, trying to pull my mind out of the gutter.

"Addy, how drunk are you?" he asks, taking a step closer into my space.

I blink at him, running his question through my mind. "Not that drunk," I whisper.

He pushes a fallen tendril behind my ear and rests his hand over my pulse that's fluttering so fast I know he can feel it. "What if I wanted to kiss you?" he whispers.

This is like a dream come true for me. I press up on my toes and seal my lips over his. It's perfect, and they are just how I remember. His breath tastes like the gin and tonic he's been drinking, and it's all the more intoxicating. He wraps his large hand around the back of my neck and pulls my body flush with his as he deepens the kiss. My heart is hammering out of my chest as I fist the lapels of his suit jacket, trying to get closer to him.

He pulls back all too soon, and I'm breathing heavy. He drops his forehead to mine and whispers, "Sorry."

I look directly into his eyes. I need to know this isn't a dream, that I didn't make this up because I want it so fucking bad. I've wanted him since I met him. "Ethan."

He drops his arms from me and turns, giving me his back. The heated moment passes, and I want to cry. My heart aches as he steps away from me and drops his head to his chest. "I'm sorry, Addy. We shouldn't have done that."

I reach my hand out for him, but he moves away further. My chin quivers as I fight back the tears that want to fall so badly. The ultimate rejection. I didn't think it would hurt as bad as it does. I square my shoulders and raise my head. No one is going to make me feel this way.

"I'll catch my own ride home for the evening." I turn on my heel and leave him standing there, alone.

The sad part is, he has no idea how much he's hurt me, or how hard it's going to be to face him Monday morning. I hear him call out for me, but I don't turn around. I gather my stuff and call for a rideshare.

CHAPTER 10

ETHAN

I pull my mask all the way off my face. It feels like I'm suffocating with it on. *What the fuck did I just do?* I was so fucking consumed with how she'd taste, I broke my own fucking rule. Don't mess around with employees. I learned that after my fuck-up of a father. She mutters something about catching a ride, and then she's at the door before I have a chance to even think this through.

"Addy, wait," I call to her, but my voice falls on deaf ears. "Fuck," I mutter, rubbing my hand along my jaw. I look around at the empty space and slam my fist against the wall. The dull ache travels through my clenched hand and up to my elbow before dissipating.

On my way back to the ballroom, a few more people stop to chat with me about possible projects. I only halfway hear what they tell me. I nod and smile where appropriate and ask them to contact me at the office as I hand over a business card.

I walk back into the ballroom, and Roxanne glares at me. *Yes, I know, you probably hate me right now.*

"Roxanne, do you know where Addy went?"

"She told me she wasn't feeling well and was heading home early. Blamed it on something she ate." She crosses her arms over her chest.

I don't miss the icy glare she gives me. I'm sure she saw right through that bullshit, being her friend and all. Cal offers a sympathetic shrug.

"I'll leave the car for you two to get home. I'll call a rideshare. Enjoy your evening." I turn to look at Cal. "I expect you to get her home safe."

He puts his hand over his chest and feigns shock. "I've been a perfect gentleman all evening." He smirks. "She'll be fine. I'll get her home."

I nod and head out the door to catch my ride. Before ordering it, I went back and forth on which address to use, but I know I made the right choice as the driver pulls up and I climb in the back. The ride is silent, which I'm thankful for. When I look up to her apartment floor, all the lights are off. It's been about an hour since she left, so maybe she's in bed, asleep.

Addison: *Can you come get me?*

My heart pounds. She told me she was going home. Where the hell is she?

Me: *Where are you?*

Addison: *RISE.*

What the fuck is she doing there? I don't have time to ask questions. She needs to get out of that place. I call for another ride and send a small prayer up that it's around the corner. I hop in the back.

"I will pay you an extra hundred bucks in cash to get me to *RISE* in under twenty minutes."

He gives me some disgusted look in the mirror, which I choose to ignore, and floors it. *Money always talks.* I text Addy to tell her I'm on my way as my leg bounces with nervous energy. I pull at the tie knotted around my neck, trying to find the air to breathe. A million questions are running through my mind, starting with why the hell she would go there in the first place.

I swear to God, if some asshole has touched her in any way, I'll kill him. The guy pulls up to the front door and stops. Fifteen minutes, that might be a new record. "Wait here. I need a ride back. I will be right back."

"Man, I've got other rides I can get."

I growl deep in my throat. "Trust me, I'll make it worth your while. Here's the hundred." I hand him a bill. "I've got a matching bill if you wait, and I'll give you a five-star review."

The guy's eyes light up as he nods. I climb out and look at the bouncer. He doesn't even ask who I am and pushes open the door for me. Someone must have told him I was on my way to get Addy. Right inside the door, two girls are waiting, and my eyes lock with Addy's. *Jesus.*

She's in stripper clothes. Where the fuck did she get stripper clothes from?

"Mr. Freeman? I'm Madam Isis—"

"Why is she dressed like that?" I snarl, pointing to her clothes. *Something about this whole thing seems oddly familiar.* Addy is dancing up against the girl, grinding into her leg with a wide smile stretched across her face. Madam Isis doesn't seem too concerned about her dancing.

"She's drunk and needs to get out of here. I trust you can take her home safely?" She raises her eyebrows in challenge.

She still hasn't answered my question, which is starting to

piss me off. "Why is she here, and who the hell gave her those clothes?"

"Now's not the time to talk about this. Please get her home safe. I can't do it; otherwise, I would." Addy kisses the girl on the cheek and whispers something in her ear. Madam Isis rolls her eyes and walks her toward me, handing her off.

Addy snuggles into my side and closes her eyes as she sways to the beat. *What the fuck are you doing, Addy?*

"Can you walk?" I ask her, pushing her hair out of her face.

She looks up at me lazily and takes a step, but almost goes down. I scoop her up in my arms, and she snuggles into me.

"You smell so good," she says quietly, and I smile down at her.

"So do you," I whisper.

We step outside, and the driver gets out to look at the two of us. "She's passed out drunk and a friend. Open the damn door," I yell at him. After some rearranging, she's lying down, her head in my lap as I gently stroke her hair on the way to her house. I open her purse to locate her keys when the guy pulls up. I lift Addy into my arms and walk to the elevator.

She blinks her eyes open and looks at me. The biggest smile covers her face, and my heart pounds in delight. She's so beautiful when she smiles like that.

"Hey, beautiful," I say. She won't remember this in the morning anyway, and it feels good to finally get it off my chest. "What were you doing at the strip club tonight?"

"Dancing," she says with a sigh as she closes her eyes and turns into my chest. "Do you want a private show?"

God, the thought of her in that skimpy outfit giving me a private dance turns me to steel. "Not tonight, babe." I unlock her front door and walk down the hallway to one of the bedrooms. When I try to put her down, she holds me tighter, refusing to let go. She's strong, that's for sure.

"Addy, let go. You're in your bed." Her grip relaxes, but she opens her eyes and looks at me. She reaches her hand out, and I allow her to touch my face. "Get some sleep. I'll see you on Monday."

"Don't leave me," she whispers. "Please."

"Why didn't you come home right away? Why did you go to *RISE?*"

"I told you, I wanted to dance." She yawns and turns, giving me her back. "They like me there. That's where my friends are," she mumbles.

I can't stay here, but I don't want to leave her, either. I'm not even sure what the hell she's talking about, but I know she's drunk and is going to have a massive headache in the morning. I look down at her and pull the blanket over her petite form. I sit at the edge of the bed and hunch over, placing my head in my hands.

I fucked this one up pretty bad. She twists under the blanket and faces me, her eyes closed and features relaxed. I want to crawl into bed with her, but that would be a horrible mistake, wouldn't it?

She needs me. Or it's what I tell myself as I kick my shoes off, undo my pants, and take my shirt off. I crawl into the bed beside her and pull her to my chest. Her breathing is deep and even as I stroke her hair and kiss the top of her head. She turns again and presses her ass into my front before she settles down again.

This is going to be a long night. I close my eyes and let sleep pull me under.

CHAPTER 11

ADDISON

My mouth feels like it's been stuffed with cotton, and my head is throbbing so much I feel like someone is beating a bass drum inside my brain. *What the hell did I do last night?* I groan when the night comes flooding back to me. The kiss, showing up at *RISE* to dance and possibly get laid. Everleigh put a stop to that real quick. *Bitch.* I just needed to forget about his dumb ass for a little while, and she stepped in.

The one thing I can't remember is the ride back home. Surely, I didn't drive. She never would have let me go. I reach my hand out and pat the end table in search of my phone. My hand knocks into a bottle and knocks it to the ground.

"Ugh," I moan as I force my eyes to open. They feel as if they are super-glued together, and it takes me an extra minute to make them work. I find my phone and unlock it, the light from the screen momentarily blinding me, and I groan in agony.

Note to self, don't drink that much without food again.

I have half a dozen messages from Eden, worried about me

leaving the ball so abruptly, but the one that makes my heart stop is the one waiting for me from Ethan.

Ethan: *Good Morning. I left some aspirin and water by your bed. If you read this before I get back, I went to get coffee and something greasy.*

What the hell does he mean by "get back"? I see a few messages to and from him from last night, and I scroll up to read them. I squeeze my eyes shut and scrunch my face as I try to remember sending the messages, but I can't.

Which means I didn't send them. Which means Everleigh did to get my ass home before I did something stupid. I shake my head and regret it as the world around me spins. I slowly sit up, grab the bottle from the floor, and take the aspirin on the table in hopes of it being an instant cure for the headache.

I hear the front door moments later and pull on the closest t-shirt I find so I'm somewhat decent. I catch a glimpse of myself in my closet mirror, and I'm horrified. I look like death warmed over. I wipe some of the stray makeup from under my eyes and pull open the door.

I gasp and jump as Ethan stands there in his suit from last night. "Jesus, Ethan, you scared me."

He lifts one side of his lips into a smirk, and damn if it's not the sexiest look ever. I press my thighs together and give myself a quick mental talk about keeping it together. "Sorry, I wanted to let you know food and coffee are here if you're up for it." He glances down at my Rolling Stones shirt and then back up to me. "Do you have the moves like him?"

I glance around me, not understanding what he means. "Like who?"

He gives me a full-on grin, and I nearly come right there.

"Jagger. You know, moves like Jagger?" He asks in reference to the song.

My lips part to form an O. "My moves are way better than his," I mumble as I brush past him in favor of the greasy food I smell from the kitchen.

"I didn't know what you liked, so I got a few things, and also something healthy in case you wanted that instead."

We both sit, and I open the bag to inspect the contents. I settle on a bagel egg sandwich with cheese and ham. I unwrap it and dig in. I'm starving after not eating a lot last night and then dancing on stage.

I lower my food and watch him chew. He must feel my eyes on him because he looks at me, swallows, and says, "What?"

"Why are you here?"

He takes a sip of his drink, buying time before he gives me an answer. "You asked me to stay." He holds his hands up in front of him defensively when I open my mouth to deny it. "I kept my clothes on, and nothing happened."

I know nothing happened. If something had, I'm sure my subconscious wouldn't have blocked out such a momentous moment. I've been waiting nine long years for the chance to be with Ethan Freeman again.

"I know."

Relief washes over him as his shoulders slump. "Addy, we need to talk about last night."

I tense and freeze with my food halfway to my mouth. "I know, it was a mistake. I'll pretend nothing happened. You don't have to worry about it. I won't tell anyone. I was a little drunk, too. I should have stopped it before it happened." The lie spews from my lips.

He pushes out a breath. "I was actually talking about why you were at *RISE*."

"It must have been on my mind since you asked me about it

recently. I figured no one would look for me there, and I could have a few drinks." *I definitely fucked up by going there last night.*

"How did you get the stripper clothes?"

My heart beats a little faster, and I swallow hard, trying to compose myself. Times like now I wish I was a better liar. I shrug and play it off the best I can. "It really doesn't matter, does it?"

He narrows his eyes at me. I know his signature move all too well. He'll bide his time and wait for the truth to come out. A sudden sharp knock on my door makes me jump. I get up and open the door to find my three best friends standing there. I really don't have time for this. I half-close the door to keep their prying eyes away from Ethan at my kitchen table.

"I don't have time for this right now. Can we talk later?" I beg in a hurried whisper.

"Addy, what the heck is wrong with you?" Lia asks. *Lia.* Out of all the people, she was the last person I expected to be mad at me right now.

"Listen, Ethan's inside, and I don't want to talk about this now. We'll talk later."

Ethan pulls the door open behind me and looks at the four of us. His eyes land on Lia, and he smiles as he places his hand on the small of my back. My body tingles at the familiar sensation. "Hi, Magnolia. I didn't know you were friends with Addison."

"Hi, Ethan. Yeah, we've known each other for a long time," Lia says.

He nods, his smile still in place. "Cool. Tell Landry I say hi and we'll get together soon." He turns to face me. "Addy, I'll message you later. We'll finish our discussion then. I need to get going." He turns to look at Eden. "Roxanne, nice to see you this morning."

I notice Lia and Everleigh glance at Eden, a silent question on their faces. "Okay." *Thank God this conversation can wait for a while.*

"Ladies," he says with a nod as he slips out behind me. I watch him until he is in the elevator and the doors close, separating us.

"Looks like your morning just opened up. We need to talk." Eden pushes her way through the doorway as the other girls follow her in.

"No, really, come on in," I mutter under my breath and close the door behind me. I'm in for a real treat if the looks on their faces are any indication of how this chat will go.

The girls all take a seat on the couch, leaving me to sit on the chair next to it. I feel as if I'm on an episode of *Intervention*. Each girl looks just as mad as the last as my eyes roam over them.

I huff out a heavy sigh. "Yes, ladies? How can I help you this morning?"

"What the fuck were you thinking, Addy? You could have blown everything last night," Everleigh chastises. "If Quinlin didn't call, what do you think could have happened to you?"

I roll my eyes at her over-dramatized thinking. "Zeus was watching, like always. It would have been fine. I was going to dance, maybe get some good dick, and then come home."

"You know how important it is that we keep our identities secret. It's for our own protection, so we can live our normal lives," Eden says.

This whole situation is making me combative. I close my eyes and count to five before I give her an answer. "It's not like *no one* knows our secret. Luca and Landry know, and it's worked out fine for us so far. The only reason Ethan even came *close* to finding out last night is because Ev texted him from my phone to get me."

"Damn right I did. Your drunk ass needed to be home in

bed sleeping off your heartache, not fucking some random guy in a club."

"Girl, we're just lookin' out for ya and want you to be safe," Lia says, reaching out and taking my hands between hers.

"I appreciate all your concern, girls, but I'm fine. Last night," I sigh again and shake my head, "was just a bad night. Ethan kissed me and then told me it was a mistake. So, I wanted to throw myself a pity party for one."

"Yet, here he was this morning. Couldn't have been all that bad. So, did you finally get to fuck the infamous Ethan Freeman again?" Eden asks, a smirk crossing her lips.

If only.

CHAPTER 12

ETHAN

The whole weekend was a disaster. I tried messaging Addy a few times, but she didn't return my calls or messages. I was so pissed off I went for a three-mile run at two in the morning because I couldn't sleep anymore. This girl is a giant mystery. The more she hides the truth, the more I want to free her from it.

We also avoided each other most of this week, with me in and out of meetings, but I refuse to let another weekend go by without discussing things with her. No. It's Friday night, and we have a date, even if she doesn't want it.

I walk to the small breakroom and stop when I hear *RISE* mentioned so I can listen in. Someone says something about going back again after the great private show he had and how she was very attentive to his needs. A few guys snicker, but when I pop my head in, all chatter stops and they watch me.

"Mornin'," I say, grabbing a mug to make a cup of coffee.

"Mornin'," they say in unison. They keep looking at one another, probably trying to figure out how much I overheard. My outward appearance is calm, but inside I'm a raging storm.

I'm dying to find out if the girl he's talking about was Ember because I'll punch his fucking teeth in if he laid a hand on her. "What did the girl look like?" *If you say long red hair and a pink and silver mask, I'm going to kill you.*

He swallows. "Um, blonde-haired girl, great body, the usual."

Relief washes through me. "Sounds like a fun time." My coffee finishes brewing and I take the mug, not waiting for their replies. *Thank God it wasn't her.* Addy is sitting at her desk when I come around the corner, and I smile when she looks up at me. Her cheeks flush a light pink, and it is damn sexy to see her caught off guard.

"H-hey," she says, unsure of herself.

"Hey."

She starts rambling, telling me about new meetings she has set up with me and my team for new potential clients from the ball, but I'm not listening to any of it. All I can hear is her damn gasp of surprise as I stole a kiss from her, and I picture doing it all over again. I *need* to do it again. Once wasn't enough. No matter how much I tell her it was a mistake, it sure as hell wasn't. Not by a long shot.

I interrupt her. "I lied, Addy. It wasn't a fucking mistake to kiss you." She stops talking, her mouth hanging open in surprise. She blinks at me a few times, and I know she's trying to figure out how to deflect this conversation. I've seen her do it many times. I hold my hand up. "I know what you're going to say, and don't."

Her chest rises and falls rapidly. "What am I going to say?"

"That it *was* a mistake. But like fucking hell it was. You know it, and I know it. There's something between us." I motion back and forth with my hand.

She looks around, her face flushing deeper, then lowers her voice. "Mr. Freeman, can we discuss this in private?"

"Excellent idea. Dinner, tonight."

She starts to protest, so I hold my hand up, stopping her. "Dinner." I keep my eyes locked with hers until she finally acquiesces and nods once.

I walk back into my office with a spring in my step. *You're mine, Addison Snyder.*

IT HAS BEEN THE DAY FROM HELL. I CAN'T WAIT TO GET OUT OF here and be able to spend the night with Addison. It has been non-stop calls and meeting invites all day. The only real highlight of the day was getting a little more information on *RISE*. It's not much, but another breadcrumb is better than nothing. I'm too stubborn to let that shit go. I shut my computer down and step into the hallway.

"Ready?"

Addison's big green eyes look up at me and then back to her screen. "This isn't a good idea, Mr. Freeman."

"What's the harm? Don't you socialize with coworkers outside of work? What makes me any different? Besides, you said we should talk in private. We can have dinner at my place if that makes it more private?" *God, I'd love to have her at my place.*

She stares up at me with wide eyes and gives a subtle shake of her head. "You're the owner of the company and my boss. I'm sure there are a million things written in the handbook about not dating those you manage."

There are. I had them added when I took over, but I can always amend it later. "We aren't dating. I told you earlier, you need to eat and so do I. Plus, we have unfinished business to discuss."

Addy has the nerve to roll her eyes at me, and I want to pull her over my lap and spank her ass for it. Just the thought makes my dick twitch in my pants. I let out a low, quiet growl, and she quirks her eyebrow at me in question. She pulls her phone out of her pocket, sends a message, and shuts down her computer.

She slides out from behind her desk and walks to the elevator with me following close behind. The doors slide open in front of us, and as they close, I'm hit with the familiar feeling of want all over again. She's put herself in the corner, away from me, like a scared kitten. Her fitted black dress hugs her curves, and I'm itching to put my hands on her. I *need* her.

I step into her space, caging her in with my hands on either side of her head. She looks into my eyes, and I see her desire pooling behind her beautiful green orbs.

"What if someone catches us?" she whispers. The fact she's worried about it almost makes me laugh. Right now, the building could be on fire, and I wouldn't give a shit.

"They won't."

She places her small hand over my chest, and I swear my heart is going to explode. I see her pulse quickening in her throat and lean my head into her neck, inhaling her divine scent. She whimpers and her knees buckle ever so slightly. I reach my hand around her waist, steadying her as my lips brush against her silky skin.

"How do you do this to me?" I ask, placing a gentle kiss on her throbbing pulse. She closes her eyes and tilts her head back, a quiet moan passing her lips.

The elevator glides to a stop, and I step away from her right before the doors open. I'm so fucking hard it's painful. I want to take her home, strap her to my bed, and do all sorts of unimaginable things to her. *I bet she likes it rough.*

She stands there, frozen in place, and I put my hand on the door, waiting for her to exit. "You coming?"

She finally manages to walk out, and I wave to the security guard as I guide her out of the building, my hand on her lower back. We walk a few blocks until we stop outside of *Firefly*, and I open the door for her. The lights inside are dim, and I know she will appreciate the cloak of darkness.

I pull her seat out like a true gentleman before taking my own seat across from her. We put in drink orders, and the waiter leaves us again. The silence stretches between us until our drinks are placed in front of us. She takes a sip of her wine and looks anywhere but at me.

"Addy, how did you end up at *RISE*?"

She presses her lips into a flat line. "I told you, does it really matter?"

I fist my hand, trying to keep my anger in check. I know what happens at places like that. She's too sweet and would be used and abused there. "That place isn't safe. The guys that go to a place like that, they aren't all good."

She scoffs and takes another sip of her drink as she looks around. "It's a lot safer than you think," she mumbles.

When the waiter comes back, I could kill him for interrupting us. I glare at him, and he says something about giving us more time before scurrying away again.

"I don't want you there. I know what men do to the girls there, and it's not safe for you. Promise me you won't go back."

She narrows her eyes and pushes away from the table. She places her hands down and leans over, speaking quietly. "You can control me at work, Ethan, but you can't control what I do outside. It's none of your business." She picks up her drink and tosses the whole thing back in one swoop. "Thanks for the drink. I've got to go."

She grabs her bag and is out of the restaurant before I have time to blink.

CHAPTER 13

ADDISON

What a prick. I can't believe I let that guy kiss me
—*twice!* I climb into a cab just in time to see him exit
the building, and then I pull my phone out.

Me: *Change of plans, I will be there tonight.*

The cab pulls up outside *RISE*. I climb out and walk to the
back of the building. *Why does that man piss me off so much, yet I
want to rip his clothes off and climb him like a tree?* I type in the
code and push the door open. One of the new-hires gives me a
small wave as she fixes her top.

"Are you doing okay, Stephanie?" I ask. She looks nervous,
but I think tonight is her first night on the pole. She nods and
bites her thumbnail. "You're going to kill it out there. Lia
taught you well." I offer her a thumbs up, and she finally smiles.

All the girls who come to work for us know this is just a
stepping stone. They are using it to get through whatever
rough patch put them here, and the four of us girls push them
to better themselves. Each girl is required to take self-defense

classes, too. We don't want anyone to be in the type of situations we used to find ourselves in.

I step into the dressing room to change into my outfit for the night. I've chosen a sexy little plaid skirt, red lacy bra, and fishnet garters. I swoop my hair up under the red wig and fix it in place before deciding on pigtails. *Every man's wet dream.* I intend on getting laid tonight—multiple times if possible—and I want it to be rough. I want to forget Ethan's touch, his soft lips against my skin.

Closing my eyes, I allow myself to relive it, just for a moment. My hand slides down and over my flat stomach, landing over my throbbing clit. Just the thought of Ethan is making it hard to control my want. I give a few swipes just to keep the fire alive, then pull my hand away, leaving myself on edge.

I finish getting my makeup on and pull the mask over my face as the MC announces me to the stage. My heart beats in my chest, nerves taking over as they do every time I stand on the stage, waiting. Then the lights come up and everything is right with the world. I scan the audience like I do every night I take the stage, looking for my next victim.

The song ends a few minutes later, and the crowd is going wild. I have several men who look like they are interested, and I couldn't be happier. I fix my bra into place offstage, and one of the girls tells me I have a private dance lined up. I can't wait to see who the lucky man is going to be. I smooth my skirt just outside my room and open the door.

Ethan.

My blood boils and I clench my jaw to keep myself from screaming at him. I take a deep breath in through my nose and push it out slowly. "Mr. Freeman, how can I help you?"

His lips turn up in a smile, but it's anything but happy. His eyes burn into mine, and I fight the urge to walk over to him and slap him across the face. "Hello, Ember. I enjoyed your show tonight." He eye-fucks me, and it makes my insides clench. *That's right, babe. You know you want me.*

"Thank you. Are you looking for a private dance, or...?" I trail off, leaving what I really want unsaid. I want to take out all my anger and aggression on him, especially because I can actually use the man who has made me angry in the first place. He doesn't know when to leave well enough alone.

"Turn around."

I want to fight him, but I need this so I do so without hesitation. He walks up behind me, presses his chest to my back, and wraps his arm around my waist, holding me against his hard body. His warm fingers graze my skin, eliciting goosebumps. I push out a shaky breath as his lips come down on the back of my neck. The kiss is gentle, but the way my body heats up under his touch is anything but.

He pushes me down, and my hair falls over my shoulders. I'm bent at the waist, my hands on the bed in front of me. "Ethan," I moan as his hands run up my legs.

"You've been a naughty girl, Ember," he tsks as he slides his hand into the front of my panties. His fingers brush over my clit, and I drop my head forward in pleasure. "You're soaked. Have you been thinking about fucking me?"

"Yes," I moan, unable to deny the truth. He grinds his cock into my ass, and I'm about to come standing here. *Jesus, this is so much hotter than I thought it would be.* I reach back, trying to touch him, but he grips my wrist, holding it against my lower back. "Please let me touch you."

His thumb slides over the scar on my wrist, and I try to pull away from him, but he's too strong.

"No," he gasps. He holds my wrist tighter, examining the scar, then brushes some loose strands of hair off my neck, exposing the phoenix tattoo all us girls have. He spins me around and looks into my eyes, pushing the mask up. I don't stop him because he's already figured it out. My face heats in shame. I'm not ashamed of what I do, or the business I own. I'm ashamed that he had to find out this way. "Addison?"

I bite my lower lip as he stumbles away from me in shock. My hand slides up to my wig, and I pull it off to hold in front of me, exposing my natural brown hair. I have never felt as small as I do right now. I can't even look at him. I keep my eyes trained on his shiny shoes.

"Jesus Christ, Addy. What the *fuck*?" He steps forward, stopping directly in front of me, his chest grazing mine. "You were going to let me fuck you? Let me think you were someone else entirely?" I stare at his shoes, not sure if I should give him an answer or not. When I don't offer any response, he snarls, "Fucking *answer me*, Addison."

I snap my head up, narrow my eyes, and cross my arms under my breasts. His eyes flit down to my breasts as they press up, then back up, giving me his full attention. "When I'm here within these walls, I'm Madam Ember. My mask, my wig, and my outfit are part of a role I play. You came here to fuck Ember." I shrug my shoulders. "What's the difference if she turns out to be me?" My response is cold—calculated.

The fire in his eyes dims and he sighs. "Get changed. You're coming with me. I'm not leaving you here."

I shake my head. "Ethan, I can't. I have another set tonight."

He clenches his hands into fists by his sides, the veins in his forearm bulging with the movement. His face reddens as he clenches his jaw in anger. "Fuck, Addy. Don't I pay you enough? I see the clothes and the nice shoes you walk around the office in. Is this a side hustle or some shit to afford all that?"

Now it's my turn to clench my jaw. *It hurts he thinks I do this to afford my lifestyle.* I stick my finger out, poking it into his chest. "You know nothing about my life or why I do this. And if you want an honest answer, no, it's not some side hustle." I throw my hands up and motion around us. "I own this fucking place, and I take a lot of pride in running it and being part of it. We built it from the ground up and made it successful."

Oh shit, shit, shit. I can't believe that just came out of my mouth. I see the gears turning in his head. I know Ethan Freeman. He reads people, and right now, he's just figured out the biggest secret I've been keeping from everyone.

"You *are* paying for my membership. And I've read there are four of you that own this place. Roxanne, Magnolia, and your other friend are the owners, aren't you? That's how you were able to get on stage and get a costume the other night," he scoffs like he can't believe it and tosses his hands up in defeat. "Jesus. Landry's kept this shit from me the whole damn time?"

I reach out for him. "Ethan, you can't tell anyone about this. No one can know, do you understand me?" I grasp his arm. When he doesn't pull away like I expect him to, I take that as a good sign.

"I'll wait for you to be done for the night, and then you owe me an explanation. You're not getting out of it this time, Addy. When are you done?"

I keep my voice down. "In about an hour."

"Meet me out front then." He stops with his hand on the doorknob, then turns to look at me. I expect him to shake his head in disapproval, but he surprises me instead. He stalks over to me, curls his hand through my hair, and holds my head as his lips crash down hard on mine. It's so unexpected that it takes my breath away.

As I gasp, he takes the opportunity to slip his tongue in my mouth and I moan in pleasure. *Yes! This is my ultimate fantasy.* I wrap my arms around his neck and pull my body flush against his. He's rock hard, and I can't help the thrust of my hips, just to feel him between my legs. I'm still wound so tight. I need him.

He pulls back and drops his forehead to mine, and we both breathe for a moment, staring into each other's eyes. "You're mine, Addy, and I'm going to prove it to you."

CHAPTER 14

ETHAN

J esus *fucking Christ.* How the fuck did I never put two and two together? I feel like a fucking idiot for not seeing it sooner. I pull my phone from my pocket and hover over Landy's name for what feels like the fiftieth time in the past hour, wanting to rip him a new asshole for not telling me this sooner. He knows all about Ember. I unloaded that shit on him one night after having one too many drinks. It was right before Addison started working for me.

Deep down, somewhere, I must have known. It can't be a coincidence that I fell for the same girl without knowing it. The woman I've been dreaming about for almost ten fucking years has been in front of me this whole time, and now she's my assistant. The one who drives me crazy in the office, walking around in those skirts and dresses. *The fucking temptress.* I slam my hand on my steering wheel as I look around like a crazed person.

My mind hasn't stopped since I left her in the club. I glance at the clock. If she's not out here in five minutes, I'm going to go in and drag her ass out. My hand twitches at the thought of having to teach her some manners. I remember my time with Ember—Addison, from all those years ago, and no pussy has ever felt so damn good wrapped around my dick. I never did go back after that night, though. I couldn't bring myself to see her again, to take that from her again, as much as I wanted to. *I was too chicken shit because she was a Goddamn stripper. What would the public and potential clients think?*

I lean my head back against the headrest and close my eyes, still trying to wrap my mind around all of this. Then I think back to the last conversation I had with Ember, the first time I went back to the club, just a few weeks ago. I mentioned my father, and she got defensive, saying he's not allowed back there. *What the fuck did he do to her?* My nostrils flare as I think of all the horrors he possibly inflicted on her.

A sudden tap on the window startles me, and I open my eyes to see her standing by the passenger side, biting her lip. She looks so damn innocent when she does that. I've seen it in the office a hundred times, and I want to pull it between my teeth instead. I roll down the window. "Get in, Addison." I keep my voice calm and even, despite the war that's raging within.

"Give me your address. I don't want to leave my car here overnight," she says. "I'll follow you."

I'm not stupid and she knows it. "You didn't take a car here. You came in a cab, remember?" She narrows her eyes, thinking I forgot. "And then I'll have to come to your apartment and drag your ass over my knee because you don't know how to follow damn directions." She smirks and her eyes light up just a fraction. *I knew she was kinky.* I want to drag every fantasy out of her, show her she wants me just as bad as I *need* her.

She opens the door and slides in without another word. I take off as soon as she closes the door, needing to get her to my place as quickly as possible. The air crackles around us, charged with sexual tension. I lay my hand on her thigh, testing the waters. When she doesn't push me away, I slide my hand up a little further. Her leg feels like silk under my touch as I push her skirt up, stopping just before her panty line. She still has the damn fishnet garters on, and I'm surprised I haven't come in my damn pants. She breathes out a shaky moan and reaches for me.

I place her hand over my hard cock and thrust my hips up as she gives it a tiny squeeze. She needs to know how I feel, how much I want her. "That's what you do to me, Addy. You've been doing this to me since you started working with me. You show up in the fucking skirts or dresses and those fuck-me heels every damn day. They make my cock ache."

She whimpers so quietly I'm not sure I heard her. I watch from the corner of my eye as she licks her lips and pulls my hand higher so it's resting right over her exposed panties. *Fuck me.* Lazily, I rub her clit over the flimsy material, and she spreads her legs, giving me more room. No words are spoken between us, but none need to be said right now.

I pull into my driveway and thank God for small miracles. I get out, run to the other side, and open the door for her. Taking her hand in mine, I rush inside, needing to get us both out of these clothes.

I pull her inside, spin her, and slam her back against the wall. Her breath leaves her in a whoosh, and my lips are on hers again. She presses her hips forward, rubbing herself on me as I press my tongue in, deepening the kiss, taking everything I need from her. I dig my fingers in her hair and wrap the tendrils in my fist, moving her head how I want her. She claws at my shirt with her tiny hands, trying to pull it off. Her whines of protest have me pulling away from her.

I'm trying so damn hard to control myself and not fuck her against this wall. I stoop down and toss her over my shoulder like she weighs nothing, and she lets out a giggle of surprise as her hand lands on my hips, keeping herself from smacking into me.

"Ethan, I can walk," she protests, squirming in my grasp.

My hand comes down hard over her left ass cheek, and she gasps, clearly not expecting that. "That's for lying to me." She tries to say something, and I do it again. This time she moans and drops her head, relaxing. "That's for teasing me." One more time, my hand comes down, this time harder and on the opposite cheek. "And that's because it turns you on."

"Ethan," she moans as I place her on her feet inside my bedroom. I slide the zipper down on her dress, and it pools on the floor by her heeled feet.

She tries to kick her shoes off, and I shake my head. "Leave the fuck-me heels on. When you wear them at work, you can think about how good I fucked you and made you come." She's standing before me in a black lacy bra, matching panties, and black heels.

She drops to her knees in front of me and looks up with her hands on my belt. "Please, Sir," she asks permission. *Oh, fuck me. No way she knows how long I've dreamed of hearing her say those words.*

"Fuck, Addy." I wrap my hands around her hair and tug her head back, forcing her to look up at me. "Are you going to be a good girl and suck my cock?"

When she nods, I release her. She fumbles with my belt for only a moment before pushing my pants and boxers down past my hips. She reaches out and touches my throbbing cock, sliding her tiny hand up and down the shaft, barely able to close her fingers around it. She leans forward and wraps her lips around the tip, her tongue teasing the underside.

I've jerked off to this fantasy so many times over the last few years, but this, this is better than anything I could have ever come up with. Her mouth is warm and wet around my cock, and her fingers feel like silk as she works my shaft like an expert. My fingers deftly undo my shirt buttons, and I toss it on the floor in the corner. My pants are still around my ankles, but I'll remedy that in another minute.

Wrapping my hand in her hair again, I hold her in place as I start using her mouth. I watch her fingers dip down inside her panties as she touches herself in return. "Gonna be my good fuck toy, Addy? Gonna let me use your holes as I need them?" She moans around me, the vibrations making my balls lift. There's no way I'm not going to be buried balls deep in her when I get off, though. "Such a dirty girl," I mumble.

I pull her off me. "Bed, now. All fours." I help her stand, and she does exactly as I ask, lifting her perfect ass in the air, giving me the best damn show I've ever seen. I admire her for a minute, watching her pant with need. Wetness travels down her thigh, and I stick my tongue out to lap it up.

"You taste better than I thought you would." I pull her panties down, and she lifts her legs, allowing me to pull them all the way off. I pull her hips back to my face and eat her out from behind. When she starts squirming in my grasp, I spank her ass, hard. She rears up on a gasp of surprise, and I watch her beautiful skin flush from the hit.

"Ethan, it's too much," she mewls.

"Then come on my face like a good girl," I say before diving back in. Her hips rock back into me, and when I insert two fingers, she tenses around me and drops her upper body, riding out the waves of her orgasm. I'm on auto-pilot. I couldn't stop even if I wanted to. I kneel behind her and thrust hard while she's still coming, and she squeezes me like a vise.

I don't take it slow. I fuck her hard and fast, her hips slamming back against mine each time I thrust forward. I grip her hips, my fingers indenting her creamy flesh as I take out all my anger and aggression on her little body. She doesn't fight it;

she gives in, and I'm on the edge when she starts squeezing me again.

"I'm going to come again," she pants.

I want her begging. "Ask nicely," I grit as I rut into her, my own orgasm close.

"Please, Sir. Please, can I come?" She pants as she looks over her shoulder at me. Her green eyes lock with mine, and I'm done for. She doesn't know it, but she owns every fucking part of me. There's nothing I won't do for her. She's still waiting for my response.

"Come, Addison."

She digs her fingers into the sheets and grasps them as she inhales a deep breath. The moment she starts clenching around me, I pull out and finish on her back, panting and moaning as streams of hot cum land on her, marking her.

She collapses and looks over her shoulder at me as I get off the bed and walk to the bathroom to get a towel to clean us both up. I'm still semi-hard as I walk away from her, even after that mind-blowing experience. I clean myself up, then wipe her back before getting into a pair of boxers and sweatpants. She lays there sated, and I hate to be the one to ruin this moment of bliss.

"Addy, we need to talk."

CHAPTER 15

ADDISON

I knew it was coming sooner or later, but I hoped we could have enjoyed post-sex bliss for more than two seconds. He's right, though. Ethan Freeman won't stop until he's had his questions answered. I've seen it time and time again at the office. I stand and look around for my panties. When I spot them, I pull them up over my hips and into place. Ethan's eyes never leave my body, and I blush under his gaze.

I reach for my dress, and he pulls it out of my grasp, offering me a t-shirt and a pair of boxers instead. I take them and pull them on as I kick my heels off. He takes my hand and leads me to the couch to sit.

"Can I get you something to drink?"

A glass of whiskey would be nice. I'm sure I'll need it for his interrogation. "Whatever you're having."

He comes back a minute later with two bottles of water, a bottle of scotch, and two glasses. *Close enough.*

I take the water and take a large gulp before putting it on the table, waiting for his questions.

"Why?"

"Why, what?" I ask.

"Why have you been paying my dues? How long have you been paying them?"

I press my lips together and take a deep breath. So many memories I'd rather forget flood back. My start in this world is one I would rather forget, but at the same time, it has made me who I am today. I wouldn't change that for anything. I'm strong and can handle anything life throws at me.

"*RISE* opened about eight years ago. All of us girls used to work at *The Devil's Playground* before it burned. As you know, the clients that visited there weren't always the... nicest. The owner was an asshole, too."

"Vince Perelli, right?"

I nod. "When we opened the club, we knew we wanted to control who was allowed in, and who wasn't. It became a members' only club from the beginning. That way we can control and vet the members, and it keeps all of us girls safe."

I don't want to tell him I've been paying them because I've been in love with him since the moment he fucked me nine years ago, but there is no way around it. He lifts his eyebrow in question, waiting for me to answer the second question he asked.

"You treated me like a person that night, and as little as it probably meant to you, it meant a lot to me."

"You've known who I was this whole time?" he asks.

I nod and reach for the tumbler of scotch on the table. "I found out who you were shortly after that night, yes."

He rests his forearms on his knees and bows his head. "And you work for me, knowing we had sex and I had no clue who you were."

I nod again. "I found out who you were and changed my course of studies to get my MBA. I researched your company, well, your dad's company, and knew it would be an amazing place to work one day. That was my goal. I never expected to be given the role as your executive assistant."

His eyes darken when I mention his dad. "What did that bastard do to you?" The words are full of malice and hate.

I choke on the scotch and cough, the burn sliding down my throat. I shake my head and keep my features calm. "Nothing…" I trail off. I can't tell him what he tried to do. Not yet. Maybe if things progress, we can go down that road, but until then, it's another one of my secrets.

He eyes me up and down. I'm not stupid and neither is he. He knows there's more I'm not telling him, but thankfully he lets it slide. I study him, watching all the small movements he makes. He's so different from the man I see at work every day. Here, he's relaxed, and even though I just dumped a ton of information in his lap, he seems to be processing it well.

"So, what now?" I ask, hoping I didn't just lose my job over this. If so, I'd find a way to make it work; I always do. My mind drifts back to how I even got started at the strip club. Eden had been distant the first moment I met her freshman year when she was my roommate. After a rough night, we confided in one another, and I told her I couldn't find a job. I can still remember the day I showed up at the club like it was yesterday.

The Devil's Playground. This couldn't be right. I looked at the number above the door and back to the address Eden had given me. This wasn't a bar; it was a strip club. She had to be out of her fucking mind. Eden stepped through the front door, out into the sun, and when she spotted me, she waved.

I was beyond pissed. I got out and slammed the door behind me, then marched straight up to her. My body shook from the adrenaline coursing through my veins. "Are you fucking kidding me?" I gestured to the red sign on the side of the building. "This is the bar?"

"Addy, please, just listen to me." She batted her hands in front of her, willing me to calm down.

I crossed my arms over my chest, my lips pressed into a tight line. "You have one minute."

"You're never going to be able to get another job. It's either here or nowhere." Her cheeks burned red, and she kept her eyes on the ground. "You'll be safe, though. I'll make sure of it."

I shook my head back and forth in disbelief. My chin quivered as I pulled my bottom lip between my teeth to stop from crying. How did my life end up like this? What did I do to deserve it? She placed her hand on my shoulder, and I saw the unshed tears in her eyes. She didn't want this for me any more than I did. Eden Riser was a pawn in this game, just like me.

"You promise I'll be safe?" I whispered, a tear rolling down my cheek. She nodded as I wiped my eyes with my arm. "How?"

"Because I'm the only one who knows his weakness."

The door behind her opened, and Lia and Everleigh stepped outside to join us. They were in sweatshirts, just like Eden, but their legs were bare. Everleigh offered a smile and waved while Lia stared at me. I wasn't sure what to make of her yet, but Everleigh seemed nice.

I looked at Eden. "You'll teach me?"

"Everything I know."

She reached her hand out for mine. My breathing slowed as I put my hand in hers, and she wrapped her cold fingers around mine before walking me to the other girls for introductions. I felt as if I was joining a sorority or something with how serious everyone was. Don't some girls strip for fun? This was just a way to make some money until I graduated from college. So, why did I feel like I'd just sold my soul to the devil?

"Addy? You okay?" Ethan asks, pulling me from my memories.

I blink at him a few times and take a deep breath. "Yeah." I stand. I should probably get going. I'll call for a ride."

"Whoa, calm down there. You're not going anywhere." He grabs my wrist, keeping me in place. He rubs his thumb over my scar as if he's trying to figure out how I got it. Trying to learn my story from touch alone. "It's late and you need sleep. I have a spare room you can sleep in, and we can pick this up tomorrow once you've had some time to sleep on it."

I try to protest and he glares at me, daring me to defy him. Finally, I nod as he shows me to the room, not that I was expecting to be able to sleep in bed with him. He tells me goodnight and I settle into the large, soft bed.

God, the sheets smell like him. Everything smells like him, causing sensory overload. Every time I close my eyes, I see him behind my lids and feel him on my skin. I punch the pillow and turn to the side, trying to find a comfortable position. This isn't good. I'm in way deeper than I thought, and if I'm not careful, I'm going to drown.

My life was so much simpler before I blurred the lines. He never should have found out. I never should have told him. He's never going to look at me the same way. Now, when he sees me, he's going to see Ember, just some random stripper. I pull my phone out and text Lia. Landry got a huge surprise when he found out who she was, and that she was pregnant with his baby. A miracle, really. I know she'll have some insight on what to do.

Me: *Hey, are you up?*

Lia: *Yeah, what's going on?*

Me: *Ethan knows. If he hasn't gone to Landry yet, it's only a matter of time. Can I spend the night over there?*

Lia: *I'll leave the front door unlocked. You've got a lot to tell me in the morning.*

I climb out of bed and walk down the hall to Ethan's room. I hear his even breathing and quiet snores coming through the door. I feel guilty for leaving like this, but I don't think I can handle another round of questions from him in the morning, and I know he will come looking for me at my apartment.

I need some time to sort this out. I'm going to need a night with the girls before I can see him again.

CHAPTER 16

ETHAN

I kick the covers off me and stare at the ceiling. The sun is barely peeking through the blinds, so it's still early. My mind has been reeling since learning all the new information Addison dumped on me last night. I have so many more questions for her, but I know if I push too much too soon with this, she's going to pull away. The girl I've wanted for years has been right in front of me, and I've been too stupid to do anything about it—too scared.

Not anymore.

Even when she first came to work for the company, there was something special about her, but I looked past her. Too wrapped up in taking over the company, too wrapped up in fixing all my dad's fuck-ups. I didn't have time for a relationship. Over the years, it just became who I was. If I needed a date, I would find one. Depending on how it went, we might get a hotel for the night, but there was hardly ever a second date.

Addison is the first woman I've brought back to my place. That should scare me, but it doesn't. In fact, it makes me really happy. I love that I've been able to share something special with her, even if she doesn't realize it.

I need to clear my head, but I don't want to leave her alone in the house. I open the door and tiptoe to the spare bedroom. My dick stands at attention, wanting to slide back into her tight heat. Memories of the way she came for me are burned in my mind. I bite my knuckle to keep from moaning out loud. We need to talk more today before I can even think about that.

I reach for the handle and peek inside the room, expecting to find her curled up in the bed, but instead, the bed is empty. The blankets have been pulled back in place, and there is no sign of her ever being there. I look down the hallway, and the bathroom door is open. Next, I march to the kitchen, but that's also empty.

Son of a bitch!

I toss on a pair of jeans and a t-shirt and haul ass to the office to see if her car is still there. When I arrive, the entire garage is empty. She must have left my place and picked it up. I pull my phone out of my pocket and try to call her.

It rings twice before she sends me to voicemail. I growl in frustration and dig my fingers through my hair. "You'd better have a good fucking reason for leaving this morning. We weren't done talking." I hang up and toss the phone into the passenger seat. I need to go for a fucking run and clear my head.

I drive home, much slower this time, and change into some shorts and a t-shirt. Whenever I need to clear my head or work through a problem, I run. It's the best way for me to figure shit out. I put on my headphones and take off, letting myself get lost in the motion.

About an hour later, I return, but there's still no response from Addison. I try calling her, get sent to voicemail *again*, and so I text her.

Me: *You owe me an explanation as to why you left. You can't hide forever. We still work together.*

I look at the time and decide it's late enough. I call Landry, who picks up on the second ring.

"Hey, man, what's up?"

"You've got some explaining to do. I know about Magnolia's *nightlife*," I say, annoyance lacing my words. "I think we need to meet up and chat."

He sighs. "I'm watching Aliana while Lia's out, but when she gets back, we can meet up."

"Text me when and where, and I'll be there."

"Okay. See you soon." He hangs up.

Fuck. I have so much pent-up energy I contemplate going for another run, but decide throwing myself into work might be more useful. Al Costanza sent me an email with an outline of the services he's looking for. I read it a few times, making sure I understand everything.

He's looking for extra security for servers on his company computers and even wants to be able to access a log of when employees access it. That's all fine and dandy, an easy fix, but the part that's got me scratching my head is he wants the same thing done to his home computer systems. *Why would he need this type of security on home computers?* What's he hiding?

The amount of business and revenue his company would bring is insane, and I know the board would be over the moon with this client. I could basically charge this man anything I want, and I know he has the means to pay but, but what is it going to be worth? Will I be stuck working with him forever? I suppose I could give him a trial run period to see if he likes the services. As much as I hate to admit it, I want to take a look around his computer to see if my suspicions about him are right, even though it's definitely not ethical.

My phone rings, and Landry's name lights up the screen. I swipe to answer and put the phone to my ear. "Hey."

"Let's meet at *Gusto's* in an hour. You can buy me a beer."

"Done. See you then."

I try Addison again, and when she doesn't answer, I call it quits for a while. If I can't get answers from her, I'll get them any way I can.

I WALK INTO *GUSTO'S* AND SEE LANDRY ALREADY SEATED AT A booth with a beer in front of him. He looks at me as I slide into the booth. The waitress comes over, and I order a beer as well. I have a feeling I'm going to need something after this conversation.

"How's Aliana?" I ask. I might as well get the pleasantries out of the way now, and who doesn't love talking about their kids.

His face lights up. "She's getting big, really big. You should come by the house more often to see her." He pulls his phone out of his pocket and swipes through a few pictures, showing me. "She looks like Lia. I'm sure I'm going to have to keep the boys at bay when she's older." He smiles again looking at a picture and puts his phone away.

"Congrats, man, she's beautiful."

He sighs. "Spit it out, Ethan. Ask your questions. I'm sure you've already figured it all out anyway." He takes a sip of his beer, and I wait for him to place it down before I talk.

"You knew Addison was Ember, and you never said a damn word to me. You listened to me bitch about how amazing she was. I've told you the same about Addy and how I was hard for my damn assistant."

He shakes his head and leans back in the booth, crossing his arms over his wide chest. "It wasn't my place to tell you shit, and if you remember correctly, I told you to go after Addison."

I ball my hands into a fist, trying to channel the rage growing inside me. "I can't be fucking my assistant. I told you there are rules on interoffice dating, especially for me." I scrub my hand down my face and rub the stubble on my jaw.

He smirks and shrugs. "From what I've heard, you've already fucked her." My face pales, and I take a good long swig of the beer to gather my thoughts. "She came by last night to talk with Lia, and I could hear some of their conversation this morning." My eyes light up, and he groans. "Man, I know that look. Leave her alone for a while. Give her a few days to figure everything out."

The asshole's right. I know I should leave her be, but she left my house in the middle of the night without saying a damn word to me. *It never would have happened if I wasn't chicken shit and made her sleep in my bed with me.* I could have woken her up with an amazing orgasm, then we could have showered and talked things through over breakfast.

I still have her dress and shoes in my room, which means she left in my boxers and t-shirt. I'm not sure why, but that makes me a happy man. I process what Landry has told me, and know I have to leave her be. I know Addison well enough that if she wants to avoid a subject, she will.

I spend the rest of the time talking with Landry about inconsequential things, and before long, he starts getting text messages about coming home. If the smile that spreads across his face is any indication, he's going to get lucky again tonight. Maybe they are trying for another kid, who knows.

All I know is I'm jealous as fuck of him right now. He's got the girl of his dreams, and mine keeps running away from me.

CHAPTER 17

ADDISON

This was by far the longest weekend of my life. I walked into *RISE* Sunday night fully anticipating to dance out some stress, but when I walked in, I was told he was there, waiting for me. I'm not ready to face him. Not after what we did this weekend, and certainly not after the bomb I dropped on him. I got one of the new girls to cover my shift and walked out just as quickly.

My talk with Lia turned into a pow-wow Sunday night with all the girls, and needless to say, they weren't happy he now knows. It's not like this is the first time, though. Lia went through this with Landry after sleeping with him once and miraculously getting pregnant. *I'm still convinced he has magic sperm or something.* Luca stumbled upon Everleigh's secret identity at *RISE* and kept his mouth shut. So, why should Ethan be any different?

I can trust him... right?

Lia and Everleigh were okay after our talk, but Eden was still worried and upset by the whole thing. I know Ethan, and he won't say anything to anyone. He wouldn't risk my safety or the other girls like that. He's a good man.

I've ignored Ethan's texts and calls all weekend, but as I walk through the door to the office Monday morning, I know there is no way to avoid him. *I seriously considered taking a sick day and hiding out just a little longer.* It wouldn't have done much, but I would have felt better... maybe.

I show up extra early, so he can't catch me off guard. I flip on the lights around the office, and as I reach my desk, he's standing there, waiting. I slow my steps as I approach and keep my head held high.

"Do you always stand in the dark like a creep?" I ask, putting my bag in my bottom drawer.

He holds out my dress and my shoes with a smirk. Friday night flashes through my memory, and my face heats up as I reach out to take my clothes and shoes from him. He pulls them back out of my grasp, and I narrow my eyes at him.

"Let's talk." He turns and takes my stuff with him into his office, placing them on his desk.

Damnit!

I follow behind him and close the door, giving us a bit of privacy. I stand by the door, and he walks over, flipping the lock behind me. He places his hands on either side of my head and lowers his face until it's inches from mine. My heart races, and my palms start to sweat. I know he's not going to seduce me right here, right now, but that doesn't stop my mind from playing through the fantasy.

The number of times I've pictured being bent over his desk or pressed against the floor to ceiling window overlooking Atlanta as he pounds into me is unreal. It's only gotten worse the longer I work directly under him. Especially during those late nights when he is working on something. I've pictured crawling under his desk to help ease some of his stress.

And after last night? Yeah, my fantasies are in overdrive. He was so much better than I remember. I'm sure he could make *every damn one* of my fantasies come true.

He presses himself closer, and my chest grazes him every time I breathe in. *God, he smells good.* We seem to be in a stare-off, and I refuse to go down without a fight. I didn't get where I am today because I'm chicken shit. I press my hands against his chest and try to push him away, but he's faster. He grabs my hands, spins me around, and pins me chest first against the door, pinning my hands behind me.

Oh my God, I'm soaked. This Ethan is so freaking sexy. "Ethan, get off me," I warn half-heartedly. He slides his leg between mine and pins me against the door with his body.

"You know, I thought we would have had a nice morning, but you took off in the middle of the night, just like Cinderella. You even left your shoes." *God, this is so damn hot.* I rock my hips over his thigh, needing to feel just an ounce of relief, and he groans. "That's not fair, Addison."

"You started it."

He pulls away and walks to his desk, leaving me breathless and against the door. I tuck some hair behind my ear and turn to face him. I roll my eyes when I see him leaning against the edge, looking smug.

"What do you want?"

He studies me for a minute before finally answering. "You."

I swear I stop breathing the moment he says it. How can one simple word hold so much weight?

"There are rules—"

"I wrote them, and I can change them." He walks back over to me but gives me a little more space. It's like he can't stay away from me. He takes my hands in his. "You're the only girl I've thought of in the past nine years, Addy. Now that I know your secret, it all makes sense." He chuckles and shakes his head, looking down. "I feel like such an idiot for not seeing it."

This whole thing seems like a dream. "Why not come for me sooner? Why did I have to share this secret to get your attention?"

I'm breathless. I've wanted Ethan since day one, so to hear he feels the same way is surreal. I figured I could get close to him and that would be enough. I could see him happy, and help make his life and job easier. After hearing him tell me that he wants me, I know I've been fooling myself. I've been using the club and sex as a crutch for my true desires—*him.*

He rubs the back of his neck, and the tick makes him look like a teenage boy. It's endearing. "I was scared. Scared of what my family would think, the board, all of it."

"Because I'm a stripper." It's not a question. I already know his answer.

He nods, but the look behind his brown eyes tells me he's ashamed to admit it.

I get it. I've had one boyfriend since I started stripping, and he broke up with me over something similar. He told me he would never be able to introduce me to his friends or family because of my job. What he didn't know—what no one knows except the girls—is I didn't have a choice. Vince blacklisted me everywhere in town.

I was already such a burden on my aunt and uncle after I lost my entire family in the fire; I couldn't ask them for money. I couldn't ask them to keep trying to take care of me, and I knew if stripping was the only way to make it happen, so be it. The tips weren't bad, and as long as I was willing to do private shows, I made decent money to help pay for my degree.

I was able to pile it away and then worked my ass off to get my MBA in only five years. It was hard work, but I don't regret it. By that time, *RISE* was up and running, and all of us girls had learned a thing or two about running a business and keeping the girls safe. It's so different than what we had before.

When I was at *The Devil's Playground*, nothing was off-limits. I was one of Mr. Perelli's birdies, and he liked to showcase us girls. We were the youngest ones there, and to be honest, I'm not even sure half of what he did was legal. If a customer wanted a private dance, which included a bit more, we were told to make them happy, not to say no.

My first ever private dance was with Ethan. Eden gave me a pill to slip into his drink if he started doing anything I didn't like. I was so nervous walking into the room, but when I saw it was him, I relaxed. He was so kind to me that night, and that's when it all started. The high I receive from the private shows and sleeping with men is unlike any other.

I took more private dances than the other girls, knowing how badly I wanted to finish school and find my way to working at Ethan's office. Plus, those dances taught me what I wanted in a lover, what kinks interested me, and what I didn't like.

Sex has been an outlet ever since, my drug of choice. I use it as a stress reliever. Eventually, I started using men because it was fun. *Who says only men can enjoy sex?*

"Then you started working for me. My dad fucked up his marriage by sleeping with his assistant," he scoffs. "Who knows how many other girls he's slept with, and I knew I couldn't get involved with someone I work with. It's been killing me. I want you so fucking bad my whole body aches."

He slides his hand around my waist, pulling me to him when I don't supply an answer. He dips his head, letting his breath fan across my face. There's a magnetic pull between us that's so strong, I'm not sure I'd ever be able to break it, even if I wanted to. His lips graze mine, seeking permission, and I give in. I'm not strong enough to fight this attraction, this sexual chemistry between us any longer. I've fought too long to keep my feelings hidden from this man, and I'm not going to do it anymore.

"I want you, Ethan," I moan into the kiss.

His hand squeezes my waist as he holds me flush against his body, deepening the kiss. His tongue dances with mine as we take the time to explore one another, neither of us in a rush to stop. This is heaven and hell rolled together. My body and brain wage a war with one another, and my heart doesn't give a damn.

CHAPTER 18

ETHAN

Vivid images of pushing Addy over my desk and fucking her into oblivion have me so hard. If I don't relieve this pressure soon, I'm going to come standing here. I pull her with me, backing into the side of my desk. I break the kiss and spin her around, pushing between her shoulder blades until she's bent at the waist over my desk.

"You're going to hang on tight and not make a sound. I'm going to fuck you and then, tonight, you're coming to my place for dinner. After that, I'm going to fuck you in my bed like I should have done on Friday night."

She sighs. "Yes, Sir."

Fuck! I pull her dress up over her hips and smirk when I catch a glimpse of her bare pussy and ass. She's not wearing any panties. I run my hands over her warm flesh, giving her skin a light tap with my palm. "Do you make it a habit of coming to work without panties, Ms. Snyder?"

"Sometimes. I like the rush," she says as he looks at me over her shoulder.

Sassy girl. I unfasten my belt and button, then pull the

zipper down. I reach my hand into my boxers and pull my aching cock out, slapping it on her ass a few times, and she arches her back more, offering herself to me. She is so sexy like this. She presses back against me and whimpers. I slide my finger through her folds and find her soaked, just like I thought she would be.

I thrust in hard and still, pressing my hips to hers, enjoying the feel of her squeezing me tight. I give her ass another slap before I rub the pink mark I've left on her. She moans loud, and I lean over her, my chest pressing her further into the desk.

I press my lips to her ear. "Didn't I tell you to not make a sound?" She bites her lip, closes her eyes, and nods. "Not a fucking sound; otherwise, next time, I'll bring something to gag you with." I smirk to myself. "I would have used your panties, but it seems you're full of surprises today."

Gripping her hips tight, I dig my fingers in where I'm sure she will have bruises tomorrow. Heaven. That's what it feels like being buried deep inside her. I don't know how I've survived this long without her. But I know it's only a matter of minutes before employees make their way into the office to start their busy Mondays.

"You're not going to come. Do you understand me? I want you to think about my cock buried inside you all day, and then tonight, I'll make it up to you." *I need a way to ensure she comes over tonight.* If it makes me an asshole to get off and leave her hanging for a few hours, so be it. I'm an asshole.

She nods and bites her arm, keeping a moan at bay. I thrust my hips like a crazed man. Each press forward rocks her lithe body against the hardwood desk, but she doesn't complain. I feel my orgasm starting at the base of my spine as I pound into her over and over again. She's squeezing my dick so hard I'm surprised I can keep the pace going.

"Ethan," she moans. I pull my hand back and smack it hard across her ass cheek. She rears up, and I take the opportunity to wrap my hand through her hair, holding her immobile.

"Hold your dress up higher," I demand.

She does and I pull out to shoot my cum all over her lower back and ass, marking her.

Mine.

No one is ever going to touch this girl again. Both of our breaths are ragged, and I take a second to calm my racing heart. I grab some tissues from my desk and clean myself quickly so I can tuck myself away.

"Good girl. Stay there. Let me get something to clean you up with."

I walk into the bathroom for a washcloth and come back with it, she's still bent over the desk with her feet spread apart. *Fuck, I would kill to see this every day.* I clean her up, wiping my cum off her, and pull her dress back down. I can't believe I fucked her without a condom. How could I be so stupid? *Isn't that what Landry did with Lia?*

I help her stand and she turns to look at me, lust still evident in her bright eyes. She squirms as I stare deep into her eyes. I know she can still feel me between her legs, and know she is desperate for a release. Her flushed cheeks and shaky breath are evident of that.

"Addison, are you on the pill?"

She nods. "Yeah, I'm safe and clean."

The thought of being able to have sex with her again without having to wear a condom makes me harden. *Jesus, I can't get enough of her.* She glances down at my crotch and back up at me, a bright smile on her face.

"Let's keep this between the two of us for now. Just until we figure everything out." She narrows her eyes at me, but nods.

"Dinner tonight, and I promise you won't regret it." I smile down at her as I tuck some loose hair behind her ear.

"I'll drive myself."

She walks out of my office without another word. I was going to call out to her, but it seems some people have already started to arrive, and I don't want them to get suspicious. I turn and look at the small mess of crumpled papers from where her body rested. The smell of sex lingers in the air.

It's going to be a long day.

I STOP BY HER DESK, BUT SHE'S NOT THERE, SO I CLENCH MY JAW and ball my hand into a fist. She better not have left after all that. I pull open her bottom drawer and see her bag is still there, where she placed it this morning.

"Do you always snoop through your employees' desks?" She stands in front of me with her arms crossed over her chest and her hip popped out.

"Making sure you didn't pull a Cinderella on me again," I tease.

She looks around and smirks, keeping her voice low. "Why would I do that? You promised me lots of orgasms."

"Did I promise lots? If I recall, I only said I'd make it worth your time."

She shrugs and bats her lashes at me. "If you can't deliver, maybe you're of no use to me."

I love that sassy mouth of hers. After looking around to make sure nobody is around, I grip her by her waist and pull her flush against me. She rocks her hips forward, and I close my eyes, keeping quiet. I lean down so my lips brush against her outer ear. "Addy, when I'm done with you tonight, you're going to beg me to stop, and even then, I will make you give me another. I want you coming for me and *only* me. Got it?"

She pushes a shaky breath out. "God, yes."

I take a step back before I do something I'll regret. "If you're ready to leave, I am too. You can follow me to my place since you insist on taking your own car."

She rolls her eyes and moves to gather her stuff. I walk her to her black Audi and ask her to wait for me to get mine. She doesn't seem to like my orders, but she complies anyway. *She'll be so much fun to tame.*

There's still so much I don't know about her, though. If I want her, and not just sex with her, I need to make the effort. I need to make sure her skeletons are hidden, because if anyone finds out she is really a stripper at night and I'm dating her, this company is screwed. The board already looks for any reason to get rid of me, even though I have done so much for this fucking place.

Since I've taken over, I've doubled the amount of revenue and put new products out on the market that have been gaining traction. Dad brought some negative press with him, but I've done my damned best to not follow in his footsteps. *Except for sleeping with my assistant.* I shake my head as I move through Atlanta traffic, keeping my eyes on Addy in the rearview mirror.

Finally, after what seems like forever, we pull into my driveway. I pull into the garage, and she parks behind me. I walk over to her car and open the door, extending my hand like a true gentleman. She blushes as she reaches for it and I help her step out. You would think us having sex in my office would make her blush, but no. It's a simple gesture such as helping her out of her car.

After unlocking the door, I usher her inside, turning on lights as we go. It's still bright outside, but it will be night soon.

"I know how to make a killer Penne ala Vodka. Does that sound good?" I already gave Rhonda the night off when Addy agreed to come over this morning.

She sits at the bar in the kitchen and watches me. "Sure, chef. You invited me, so whatever's on the menu."

"Well, I can tell you, you're definitely dessert."

CHAPTER 19

ADDISON

S hit like that doesn't faze me. *Ever.* Yet, when he says it, I can't stop the tightening in my belly or the blush that creeps up my neck to settle on my cheeks. He places a glass of wine in front of me, and I take a greedy sip, trying to calm my racing heart.

He looks good in the kitchen, like he should be doing this instead of his actual job. He moves around, pulling pots and pans out, then starts chopping vegetables for a salad.

"So, tell me a bit about yourself," he says, glancing up at me from his chopping.

"Wow, this feels like a backward first date or something. We've already slept together, twice, and now you want to get to know me?" I raise my eyebrow but smirk.

My past is just that. My past. I keep that hidden under layers and masks because no one needs to know the hell my life has been. Yet, at the same time, I want to tell him *everything*. If the way he looks at me is any indication, he's not going to judge. He's not trying to make me feel bad about my life or the choices I've made. It makes me feel... safe? I'm not even sure I know what that feeling is outside of the girls and the club.

I rub the scar on my left arm absentmindedly as I watch him. He notices and points it out. "How about you tell me about the scar. How did you get it?"

"Self-inflicted," I murmur before taking another sip of my wine. I see the hurt flash before his eyes, but in an instant, it's gone again. He waits for me to continue. "Tragic backstory. Isn't that what all strippers have?"

"Does it have anything to do with the few days off you take every August?"

Of course, he would notice I take the same few days off every year. I shouldn't be surprised, yet I am. I nod and, without thinking, blurt out, "I visit my family every year."

He smiles until he notices the grim expression marring my face. "Addy, what happened? Do you not get along with them?" He puts the knife down and walks around the counter to sit next to me. He hesitates, but takes my hand in his, rubbing his thumb over my scar, just like I did.

He hasn't earned this side of me yet. I may have been in love with this man for the past nine years, but he hasn't been in love with me. I can't risk putting my heart out there for him to stomp on it. No one understands the pain I went through with losing them. No one *needs* to be burdened with my pain. It's my cross to bear.

I used to have nightmares every night, reliving their deaths. Coming home to the house burning, running in after them, hoping for some small glimmer of hope. It always ends the same.

They're dead.

There's nothing I can do to change it. No matter how many restless nights, the dream is always the same. They left me. I couldn't join them, no matter how hard I tried.

His hand cups my cheek, and I blink away the memory, along with a few stray tears that have welled up as I look into his deep brown eyes. Eyes that hold so many questions. Eyes that look so understanding. "Addy…"

"How's dinner coming? I'm starved." I give him a bright smile, and he drops his hand away as if he can sense I'm not going to tell him more. And he's smart enough not to push.

I ask him more about himself, even though I know almost everything there is to know. Every date I arranged for him, I would scour the internet to find more information on her. I hang on to every word as he tells me about growing up with two older sisters and the hell they would put him through. His smile as he recounts the stories relaxes me.

I'm an addict and he's my drug.

THE HEAT FROM THE FIRE SINGED MY FLESH AS ASHEN SMOKE FILLED my lungs. I couldn't see anything, not even my own hands. I had to find them, though. They had to be here somewhere. I tried calling out and inhaled the thick black smoke that threatened to pull me further into the darkness surrounding me.

"Mom? Dad?" I managed to choke out before coughing.

I wheezed, trying to take a breath. Tears streamed down my soot-covered cheeks as I dropped to my knees. It was hopeless. I laid my head on the once pristine tile floor of the kitchen and waited for my chance to join them. I closed my eyes. My lids were so heavy, I felt as though I could sleep forever.

This was it.

I started to slip from consciousness when a pair of strong arms lifted me from the ground and cradled me against a hard chest. Something plastic was placed over my nose and mouth, and I could finally take a deep breath of pure air. I knew a man was talking to me, but I couldn't understand him. I felt the exact moment we were safe outside, as my skin erupted in goosebumps from the extreme temperature change.

"What the hell were you thinking, running in there?" the fireman chastised.

"They're gone."

I jerk awake only to be pinned down where I am, Ethan's arms wrapped around my body deep in sleep. I feel like I can't breathe, and I buck against him, trying to gain space. He's strong, his grasp on me like a vise. *No. No. No.* I dig at his arm, and he jerks awake, pulling back as I climb off the bed and tuck my knees to my chest on the floor. I rock gently, soothing my tense body and trying to let the memories slide from my consciousness.

It's been months since I've had that dream. *Months.* Things had been going so well.

"Addy, what's wrong?"

Tears sting my eyes and I close them, trying to get them to stop. I feel his warmth next to me, and my body jerks as his hands slide up and down my arms in comfort. I touch my scar, trying to ground myself.

It's just a dream.

You're safe.

He doesn't move. He waits patiently for me to talk first, and my heart feels as if it wants to explode. I fall in love with him a little more. I didn't want him to know about this, but I can't keep this to myself now, especially with the fear blanketing him. When I look into his eyes, what I see reflected back shakes me to the core. It's like he can see my demons, like he *knows.*

He holds his hand out when I look at him, and I take it as he helps me stand. I take a deep breath, hoping I'm making the right decision, hoping he won't cast me aside like so many others. He leaves the room, murmuring to stay put as I sit on the bed, returning moments later with some water bottles.

"I go home every August to visit my family."

He nods. "Right, you said that earlier."

I take a deep breath, willing my heartbeat to slow. Trying to push the words out feels like a knife in my chest. I rub the spot over my heart, willing the building pressure to dissipate. Only the girls and my aunt and uncle know about what happened to my family. I've never shared this part of my life with anyone, because no one has been worthy of it—of my pain, of my heartache.

"My family perished in a fire eleven years ago."

CHAPTER 20

ETHAN

Of all the things she could have told me, that was the last thing I expected to hear. *Jesus, I don't even know what to say to that. Sorry?* I'd sound like a fucking idiot. I reach my hand toward her in a comforting fashion as she takes a deep breath and snuggles her face into my palm.

"I woke from a nightmare I was having about that night. It's not common for me to have it, but when I do, it's usually around the anniversary of their death." She rubs at the scar on her arm absentmindedly, stuck in the caverns of her memories. She's silent again, but the hurt and anguish that cross her features are still present as she blinks. Her focus slowly returns.

I wrap my hand around her wrist, stilling her movements, making her look at me. This is the last thing I expected when I invited her to my place tonight. I figured we would have dinner, fuck, and then when we woke up, we could have more sex. Even though this isn't what I planned, it's exactly what she needs, and I want to be there to comfort her. "Tell me your tragic backstory."

She looks up at me through her dark lashes and cocks her head to the side in confusion.

"You told me every stripper has a tragic backstory. I want to hear yours."

She shakes her head, and I see the gears turning, the war she's fighting against herself. She wants to tell me, but she's stopping herself. *Okay, let's try something else to get her to trust me.*

"Okay. Would you want to come for Sunday dinner with my family?" Her body stiffens, and she takes a deep breath. "Just Mom and my sisters," I correct quickly, frowning. She has some sort of history with my dad. I know that now from how she reacted the first time I brought him up when I didn't know Ember and Addy were the same person.

She relaxes and offers a small smile. "Sure. What can I bring?"

"Just yourself. If you want to bring a bottle of wine, I'm sure they'd love you for it."

She crawls over to me and tosses her leg over my lap, straddling me. I lean back against the headboard and run my fingers up the sides of her outer thighs. Her skin is warm and soft. So fucking soft despite the muscles she has from dancing for so many years. I see the pain in her eyes—the longing for something that she will never have. I want to take that pain away.

"Use me, Addy. Use me to dull the pain."

Her mouth drops open, but she doesn't say anything. She rocks her hips over me, my growing length pressing against her covered core. She wraps her arms around my neck, and I pull her to me, sealing my lips over hers in a searing kiss. It's not gentle. It's rough. It's teeth and tongue, a fight for dominance. She needs this. She needs the control, and for once in my life, I'm willing to give it up.

She pulls my t-shirt over her head, exposing her bare

breasts, and I reach my hands out, feeling their weight before dipping my mouth to take a nipple between my teeth. She moans as she slides over me, her body shivering involuntarily. I nip and suck the bud until it is tight and she lets out another moan, dropping her head back. Her long dark hair tickles the tops of my thighs.

"Addy, can you come like this? Using my cock like this to get you off?" I bite on her nipple when she doesn't offer me a response fast enough.

She pulls in a shaky breath. "Yes, Sir."

I growl in her ear. *Those two little words...*

Jesus, she looks beautiful as she rocks over my length. I hold her hips down and thrust up, adding more friction to her clit, and she shivers again. My lips find the skin between her neck and shoulder, and I nip at it, making her gasp. Her fluid movements become sloppy as I help rock her back and forth.

"Come for me," I demand. She bites her lip and grasps my shoulders, digging her nails into my skin, no doubt leaving the markings of her pleasure behind. Her body tenses as she lets herself go on a moan, dragging herself across me, wetting my boxers in the process. She drops her head, resting it on my shoulder as I run my fingers through her dark locks.

"Your turn," she whispers, but doesn't pull her head away from my shoulder. As much as I want to get off, I didn't do this so we could be even. I feel her heartbeat match my own, calming until we both return to normal. The fuzzy edges of lust in my vision have dissipated, so I run my hands soothingly up and down her back and kiss her hair.

"Later. Can I hold you for a while?" She snuggles against my chest, nodding against it, and when her breathing evens out, I know she's sleeping peacefully again. My dick is still hard as a rock. When she shifts her weight, I bite my lip, holding back a moan. I slide her leg off me to make her more comfortable, pulling her against my chest again.

This is so fucked up. This is the last type of relationship I'm supposed to be in, yet I can't stop it. I don't *want* to stop it. Addy feels like heaven in my arms. I've been alone for so long; I can't even remember what it's like to hold someone at night. The last few girlfriends I've had didn't work out for one reason or another.

They weren't Addison. That's why they never worked out. They weren't the girl I was meant to be with.

I try to keep the thoughts at bay, but they rise up anyway, especially with my nose buried in her hair, smelling her sweet aroma. I've fought these feelings for so long, it seems like a dream that she's here—that she's mine.

She's not yours.

The little voice in the back of my brain is really starting to piss me off. *Not yet. She will be, though.* I close my eyes, hoping to dream of the sexy woman currently in my arms.

THE WEEK HAS GONE BY QUICKLY, AND I HAVE ADDY TO THANK for that. Every morning, she comes to work in a sexy little outfit that makes me want to rip it off her, and every night, I get to do just that. We haven't had sex again in the office, but that's not for my lack of trying. I've locked her in my office twice this week, hoping for a repeat, but she's kept it professional. I admire her self-control.

Sunday night comes, and I pick her up to take her to my mom's for dinner. I hope my sisters, Stephanie and Liz, don't embarrass me too much. I've never brought a girl with me for Sunday dinners, and Mom was excited when I told her I was bringing someone. I've received an array of messages in a group text between the three of them, all wanting more information.

It's been non-stop, and while it's annoying, I kind of like how excited they seem to be. Liz is my older sister and is married to Donnie. The two of them have one kid, my nephew Stevie, and Liz said he's enough. Stephanie is my younger sister. She seems to flit in and out of relationships like me, not ready to commit. The girls have been trying to set me up for months with a *nice girl*, as Mom always says.

It'll be nice to get them off my back, for a little while anyway. Donnie and Stevie won't be there tonight. Boys night out, as Donnie called it. They went to a baseball game. The boys are always my buffer from the onslaught of questions, so I anticipate I'll be screwed tonight.

When I pull up, Addy is already waiting for me. She's wearing a light pink sundress with a pair of strappy sandals. Her lean legs look amazing as she walks to the passenger side and slides in. I can't keep my hands off her.

"You look amazing, Addy." I slide my hand up her thigh and kiss her cheek, my fingers rubbing the inside of her leg. She moans and places her hand over mine, stopping my ministrations.

"I don't want to meet your mom all worked up." She smooths her dress out, and I can see how nervous she really is. She's sitting straight in the seat and is looking straight ahead.

"Addy, they're going to love you, don't worry about it." I take her chin between my thumb and knuckle, turning her face to look at me. "You're perfect." I lean over the middle console and brush a light kiss to her lips.

"What am I supposed to tell them I do for work? I can't tell them I work for you, and I sure as hell can't tell them I'm a stripper."

I shrug. "You're the best executive assistant for a big CEO.

You're very good at getting him coffee, putting together contracts, and sucking his cock," I tease. She narrows her eyes at me, and I offer her an ear-splitting grin before pulling out onto the road so we can get there on time.

She chuckles and shakes her head. "You're going to be the death of me, Ethan Freeman," she says quietly.

CHAPTER 21

ADDISON

E than's family is amazing, and I can see he inherited his charm from his mother. The whole night I've felt at ease. The only time I felt a bit tense is when they asked me about my family. Ethan was amazing, though, and jumped in for me, explaining that they aren't around anymore. His mom gave me a sympathetic look as Ethan took my hand, rubbing his thumb back and forth over the back of it. I was thankful for his support.

We are still sitting at the table, our empty bowls of ice cream in front of us. His oldest sister, Liz, is in the middle of telling us a story about the time Ethan discovered his penis could grow. He was three, and when his mom told him to get his hands out of his pants, he yelled out that he was making his penis big, for all to hear.

I look over to him as I belly laugh, and he has the good grace to blush. "Geez, it's not like I knew better," he grumbles as his face heats up. He chuckles and takes the teasing like a champ. "Why the hell would you choose to tell her *that* story anyway?" he asks.

"I could tell her about the time Mom walked in—"

"Okay, that's enough out of you. Storytime is over," he huffs, cutting her off mid-sentence.

I lean in close to him so only he can hear. "Maybe when we get back you can show me how you grow your penis." He lets a low growl pass his lips and kisses my cheek.

I miss this. I miss the teasing and the laughter of being with family. I have the girls, and we always have a great time, and they are definitely my family, but it's not the same. I don't have anyone to bring up childhood memories I've forgotten about. My heart constricts as I start thinking about my brother. Would I have been able to embarrass him in front of a girlfriend the same way Ethan's sisters are?

Girlfriend? Is that what I am, or am I just a girl he's having sex with? I pull my brows together thinking about it. It's been two weeks since he found out I'm Ember, and in that time, we've each given one another multiple orgasms and lots of sex. But we haven't put a label on it. So, am I just his friend with benefits?

Friends with benefits never goes over well. There have been way too many romantic comedies made about that, and they always end up discovering true feelings for one another. I know how I feel about Ethan, and being with him these past few weeks has solidified that. I feel the pull to him even stronger now, especially because I don't have to hide.

Everyone is still talking as I excuse myself to use the bathroom. I walk down the hall his mom pointed me to and stop to admire the pictures hanging on the wall. So many family portraits and candid moments of the kids on vacations and in the yard playing.

I don't have any of these. Nothing left of my family to reminisce on.

Ethan comes up behind me, and I'm so lost in my own

thoughts I don't hear him until he wraps his arms around my waist and places his chin on my shoulder. I wipe at a stray tear that has managed to find its way down my cheek.

"Will you take me?" His deep baritone voice cuts through the fog in my mind.

I swallow past the lump in my throat. "Take you where?" My eyes are still glued to Ethan's college graduation picture with his mom. She looks so proud of him, practically beaming standing next to him as they smile for the camera. He's in his cap and gown, holding his diploma.

"Your hometown. To meet your family."

I turn to look him in the eyes, searching for any sort of hidden motive. Why would he want to come with me? Why would he want to watch me fall apart like I do every year at their graves, begging for answers even after all this time?

"Please? You got to meet mine. It's only fair I can meet yours."

I blink and swallow again, finding it hard to get a deep breath in. "Wouldn't you rather meet my aunt and uncle? They're still alive. They took me in after the fire."

He shrugs. "I want to meet whoever you want me to. If you want to introduce me to your aunt and uncle, I'd like that." He tucks some hair behind my ear and places his hand on my shoulder. "I want you, Addy. I want to be there for you, to know all your secrets. I'll take the good and the bad as long as it means you're mine."

Mine. The one word sends a thrill down my spine, settling deep within my core. *I've been yours since long before you even knew I existed.* "What are your plans for next weekend? Maybe my boss will let me take a long weekend and we can road trip it. It's only about a seven-hour drive to Virginia." I wrap my arms around his waist, dropping my head to his chest.

"Or maybe we can just take a plane and be there in only an

hour and a half. I can have my secretary arrange it." I scoff and act offended, but when he smiles, I know he's giving me a hard time. "You tell me where, and I'll book the tickets. I'm sure I can convince your boss to give you a well-earned weekend off."

I give him a sad smile. "Thank you." I start running through the list of things I will need to bring and arrangements I'll need to make. "I just need to tell the girls so someone can cover my shift." I kiss his cheek, and he tenses under my touch. I pull back slowly to look into his eyes. "What's wrong?"

"Nothing," he says with a tight smile. "Why don't you go use the bathroom, and then we can get out of here?"

He turns me around, and I hurry down the hall into the bathroom. I look at myself in the mirror and smile at my flushed reflection. Feeling like I must be in a dream, I pinch my arm and wince with the bite of the sting. *Nope, this is real.* Ethan is real, and he's even more amazing than I thought.

We say our goodbyes, and his mom pulls me in for a tight hug. She says quietly in my ear, "Don't let him boss you around. He's a good man and needs someone strong like you to keep him straight." She kisses my cheek as she lets go of me, and I want to cry all over again. I nod and smile at her.

After trying to end my life, I lost touch with my aunt and uncle. Not because I don't love them, or because I'm not appreciative of them taking me in, but I didn't want to be a burden. Ethan's mom reminded me how much I miss having my family around. Maybe it's time to try to mend the relationship with them, too. After all, without them, there are no Snyders left besides me.

"Addy, call me anytime you want more embarrassing stories of my brother to hang over his head. It's not every day he brings a girl home, so you must be pretty special," Liz says. I look at Stephanie and see she's smiling and nodding, too.

They think I'm special? I look to him for reassurance, and he smiles down at me. He slides his hand to my lower back, and I feel sparks through my clothes. This is different than before. Before, it was lust coursing through me. This feels... lighter somehow. My cheeks flush as I pull my bottom lip between my teeth.

"Thanks. I'll keep that in mind when he's being a jerk."

He opens my car door, and I slide in before he closes it behind me then gets in on the driver's side. His body is relaxed, so different from what I normally see from him. Most of the time, his posture is stiff as if he's carrying the weight of the world on his shoulders, which I suppose he is most of the time.

"I really like your family," I say, placing my palm up on the center console. He slides his hand into mine, interlacing our fingers and smiling.

"They really like you, too. Thank you for coming tonight to meet them."

What Liz said is still rolling around in my mind. "Hey, Ethan?" He hums, waiting for me to continue. "What are we? Liz seems to think we're more than fuck buddies. I don't want to give her the wrong impression if that's what we are."

His gaze flits between the road and my face. "You're mine, Addy. You're not just a fuck buddy. I don't want you with anyone else. I want you all to myself." He brings my hand to his lips for a kiss.

Mine.

The word echoes through my mind. I've never wanted something to be true so badly in my life. He's offering it to me, so why am I so hesitant to jump at the chance?

CHAPTER 22

ETHAN

I have to call Al Costanza and tell him I'm not taking him on as a client. My dad got wind of it over the weekend and tried to sucker me into taking it, even calling an emergency meeting with the board to push for it. *Fuck that shit.* This is *my* company now, and I know what's best. Getting involved in whatever Al wants won't be good business.

I dial his number, and he picks up on the third ring. "Hello, Ethan. I wondered when you were going to call me. I spoke with your father a few days ago."

"Hi, Mr. Costanza. Yes, I'm aware. He called me after he got off the phone with you to tell me again about the services you're looking for." When he doesn't say anything, I continue. "Unfortunately, at this time, we won't be able to assist you with what you need."

His tone is casual. "Oh? Your father made it seem like it was a done deal."

Well, my father is a piece of shit. "Yes, well, as you know, he is no longer the head of this company, and while he has a seat on the board, he doesn't know all the projects we have going on. At this time, we just don't have the manpower to handle your request and provide the level of service we are known for. I appreciate you reaching out to us."

He hums in understanding. "Yes, well, thank you for the call. Say hi to *Ashley* for me. She seemed like a lovely girl when we met at the charity ball." He ends the call without another word.

Something about that statement, and him, rubs me the wrong way. If Dad wanted me to get involved with him, that can only mean trouble. Addy walks into my office a minute later, her deep red dress hugging her delicious curves, and closes the door behind her, clicking the lock in place. My lips curve up into a smile.

A locked door? This can only mean one thing.

I stand and walk to the front of my desk, crossing my arms over my chest. "Ms. Snyder, what can I help you with?"

"Well, Mr. Freeman, as you know, I am supposed to be staying late to help you with a few contracts." I quirk my brow at her. The thought of the two of us alone here makes my dick harden in my pants. With no one here, I can bring her to orgasm over every desk in this place if I want before I fuck her speechless. "Unfortunately, I have Auntie duties that came up."

Not what I was expecting. I draw my brows together in question. "Huh?"

"Lia and Landry have a last-minute date night and asked if I could watch Aliana. Eden and Everleigh are busy tonight."

"Who and who?" I assume she means some of the girls from *RISE*, but I've never heard their names before.

She blushes and clasps her hands in front of her. "Oh, um, Roxanne's real name is Eden, and Everleigh is Madam Isis. She texted you and handed me off when I was drunk after the charity ball."

I smile at her. "I figured her real name wasn't Roxanne."

"Yeah. Anyway, would it be a problem if we moved tonight to my place instead?"

I take a few steps closer and place my hands on her upper arms. I dip my head so my lips tickle her outer ear. "If you wanted me to come over, you didn't have to set up a ruse of babysitting. I can't wait to fuck you in your bed this time."

When I pull back, she's smiling up at me. "As much as I would love to tell you it's a ruse, it's the truth." She wraps her arms around me and pulls me close again. Being in her arms feels so right. Everything about her feels right. "We can head out a little early, pick up a pizza, and head to my place to wait."

She rolls her hips against me, and I stifle a groan. She has me exactly where she wants me, and she knows it. Her hand slides down my body as she gives my dick a squeeze, working it over through the fabric.

I lift her up and deposit her on the edge of my desk. I push her hand away and drop to my knees in front of her. Pushing her dress up over her hips, I press my finger against the wet spot on her panties to rub it around, inhaling her intoxicating scent.

"Is this all for me, Addy?" She nods, trying to pull me closer to her core. I lick her over her panties and slide my finger down it again. "Good girl, I love when you're wet for me."

"Ethan, either eat it or stand up. Don't tease," she says through gritted teeth.

I tsk at her. She knows by now the way to get what she wants isn't to demand me to do it. As sexy as I find it, and as much as I want to obey her every command, I'm not like that. I'm in control. I decide how this goes down. She may be able to initiate, but I'll be damned if I let her run the show.

She huffs as I stare up at her and stand. Her jaw drops open in surprise, and she stands quickly.

"I make the rules, baby. If you can't handle it, get out of the kitchen."

"Remember that tonight, handsome." She kisses my cheek and saunters out of my office, a devilish glint in her eyes. I know I'm going to be in for it later, and my rock-hard cock is screaming at me to pull her back in here, but I also want to see where she's going to take this.

———

ADDY HASN'T BEEN AROUND ALL DAY, AND I'VE BEEN GETTING A bit excited with what she has up her sleeve. I've been in and out of meetings, so not seeing her isn't that much of a shock to me anyway. She gathers her stuff as I flip off the light to my office, slinging my laptop bag over my shoulder.

I place my hand on her lower back, guiding her through the mostly empty office. I don't miss a few stray pairs of eyes watching us, and I let my hand slide away from her. I still haven't fixed that damn rule in the handbook yet, and the last thing I need is for someone to post a complaint to HR. *Even if I do own the damn company.*

She doesn't seem to notice, and when we step into the elevator and the doors close, I'm like an unrestrained animal and she's my prey. I press my arms into the wall on either side of her head, my breath fanning across her face, and I can see her pulse beating fast in the side of her throat.

"You smell so good, Addy. I can't wait to taste you," I say and nuzzle my nose into the side of her throat.

"You had a chance earlier and gave it up." She shrugs. "Not my problem." She reaches for my dick and squeezes it, drawing a moan from my lips. "Down, boy." She pushes me away in time for the doors to slide open. I didn't even realize we were that close to the garage floor, so consumed with her.

We each get into our cars and leave. She told me she was going to stop for the pizza first, so when I arrive, I lean against my car door, waiting patiently for her. She drives up a few minutes later and pulls two pizzas out, handing them to me.

This elevator ride is less heated, and when the doors open, Lia, Landry, and Aliana are standing in front of her door.

"Took you long enough to get here," Lia teases.

"Hey, this was a last-minute date. I'm doing *you* a favor, remember?" Addy says as she kisses Aliana on the top of her head. "Hey, baby girl," she coos.

Landry's eyes dart back and forth between us, and I clear my throat. "We had a contract we're working on, and she had to move it here so she could watch your kid," I clarify.

"Mmhmm," is all he says. Addy puts her stuff down and pulls Aliana from Lia's arms, snuggling into the little girl. Landry sets up a Pack N Play and puts some food in the fridge for the little girl.

Lia turns to us. "We shouldn't be too late. It's just dinner and a show." Addy quirks her eyebrow and smiles but doesn't respond. They say their goodbyes to their daughter and are practically running out the door.

"What was that about?" I ask, confused.

Addy chuckles but doesn't offer anything else. Instead, she focuses her attention on the little girl and starts playing with her. I don't think we are going to get a lot done tonight. I open a box of pizza and pull a slice out, rummaging through her cabinets to find plates and cups. Addy holds the little girl and bounces her up and down as Aliana squeals in delight.

Watching her with Aliana—the way she acts with her—puts a mental image of her holding our baby in my head. She would look so beautiful knocked up. I want to see her stomach round and firm, knowing I'm the one who made her that way. *Get a grip, Ethan.* Those thoughts should be scaring the crap out of me, not turning me on.

Addison Snyder... what are you doing to me?

CHAPTER 23

ADDISON

I finally got Aliana to go to sleep, and I feel so guilty. Ethan has been working non-stop at the table as I played with her all night. We were supposed to be working together, but any time I tried to leave her on her own, she would start fussing.

I left her with Ethan for two minutes to run to the bathroom, and when I came back, he was holding her and tickling her. I swear, my ovaries nearly exploded from the cuteness in front of me. He was so good with her. It threw me for a loop. I've never pictured Ethan with a kid before, but now that I've seen it, I can't *unsee* it.

"She's finally sleeping," I say quietly as I look at the clock. It's already nine o'clock. I never even grabbed dinner, so I'm ravenous now. I open the pizza boxes and take out a slice, biting into it like it's a filet mignon. *Oh my God, cold pizza should not taste this good.* He looks up from his laptop screen and quirks his eyebrow at me.

"Keep making those noises, and I'm not going to be able to wait until Aliana gets picked up."

I walk over to him, and he turns in his seat, facing me. I

settle in between his legs and take another ostentatious bite as I rest my hand on his thigh. "Ethan—"

A quiet knock on the door stops me, and I pull away from him to answer it. Lia and Landry are standing there, large smiles on their faces. She's wearing a long coat tied around the middle that she definitely wasn't wearing when she came by earlier.

I give her a knowing smirk. "You kids have fun tonight?" I look to Landry. "Were you a good sailor?" Lia bites her lip, nodding her head as Landry snorts a laugh. I lean close so only Lia can hear. "Any chance of me getting another niece?"

She crosses her fingers and holds them in front of her face. "Fingers crossed. We'll see."

Lia walks into my apartment and pulls a sleeping Aliana into her arms as Landry takes apart the Pack N Play. "Thanks so much for watching her tonight. I hope we didn't ruin your plans too much," Landry says, looking at Ethan.

"No, just trying to get some work done. It was no problem, man," Ethan says. They give one another a weird fist-bump, handshake thing, and I kiss Aliana on top of her head as they walk out the door, leaving me and Ethan alone. I give him a bedazzling smile and turn on my heel, walking to my bedroom.

He doesn't follow, but when I lean seductively against the wall in the living room, wearing a pair of thigh highs, garter belt, red thong, and matching bra, he perks right up. A low moan leaves his throat, and I glance down to his crotch, his bulge becoming more prominent. His feet hit the floor, and he's moving toward me before I think he even realizes what he's doing.

"Want a free show?" I pop my hip out and place my hands on my hips, giving him an unobstructed view of my skimpy outfit. He stops in front of me when I put my hand on his chest. "There are rules you need to follow, Mr. Freeman."

He licks his lips, and his Adam's apple bobs. "Like what?" His voice is deep and gravelly. I smile inwardly at how quickly I can turn him on. I turn, giving him full access to look at my backside as I point to a seat in the middle of my room.

"Sit down, Mr. Freeman." He sits and I pull some silk off my bed. "There is to be no touching... yet. Hands behind your back." He smirks but compiles. *This is easier than I thought it would be.* I tie the silk around his wrists, binding him to the chair.

"Any other rules, *Madam Ember?*" he asks as I stand in front of him again.

I turn on some music, ignoring his question, and start swaying my hips. It's been a long time since I've put on a show for someone while not at the club. It's exciting for me to have this experience with him. He's not a paying customer. He's here because he wants to be, and that thought sends a jolt of heat down my spine that settles between my legs.

His pupils are blown as I dance around him, rubbing myself against his arm, and moaning in his ear. When I reach my hand down over the bulge in his pants, he starts pulling at the restraints.

"Tsk, tsk, Mr. Freeman. You're not playing by the rules if you're trying to break free."

"Addy, please, let me touch you." He thrusts his hips up as I straddle him, holding my weight off him, brushing my covered breasts against his chest.

I start unbuttoning his shirt, ignoring his plea, and run my fingers over his muscular chest, taking in my fill of him. I grind down on him, and he tosses his head back in pleasure. I rub myself back and forth, inching my hands down his body until they settle on his belt buckle. After unclasping it, I undo the button and zipper, freeing him from his confines, then slide off his lap and kneel in front of him.

"Jesus, Addy," he groans. The corded muscles in his neck and shoulders are taut as he struggles against the bindings.

I give him a little lick, just a taste before I scoot back and settle on the floor in front of him. I spread my legs, feeling my arousal over my panties. "Since you wouldn't take care of me earlier, you can watch how I take care of myself now." His cock bounces and he groans in frustration.

"Please, Addy," he says, tugging harder at the restraints.

"Never thought I'd get to hear the big CEO Ethan Freeman beg. I rather like it. Do it again." I pull my panties to the side and rub my hardened clit how I like best, drawing my pleasure out. I lean my head against the wall but never take my eyes off him.

"Addison, I swear to God, if you don't let me out of this—"

Before he even finishes his sentence, I hear the material rip, and then he's out of his seat so fast I barely have time to move. He pulls me to my feet and lifts me like I weigh nothing. I wrap my legs around his lean waist as he presses my back against the wall. My breath leaves my mouth, but he is quick to replace it, his lips attaching to mine in a searing kiss.

I help him adjust my hips as he pulls my panties to the side and slams me down on his length. *Yes, finally.* Having him fill me is like coming home. I need everything about this man. I claw at his back, trying to gain purchase as his lips trail down to my neck. He licks and sucks at my fluttering pulse as I squeeze around him.

He groans but doesn't slow down. My breath hitches, and I don't even have time to warn him I'm coming, it hits me so fast.

"Ethan," I gasp as he thrusts hard a few more times, finally emptying into me. He holds me against the wall, both of us catching our breaths as I play with his hair. I kiss his head, cheeks, and finally his lips before he sets me down on my feet.

"You ever touch that pussy of yours again without me saying so, or you'll regret it," he warns.

I almost want to disobey just to see what the punishment will be.

"Promises, promises," I tease. "Let's get clean so we can finish work."

He pulls me into his embrace. "How about we get clean and then get dirty a few more times instead?"

"What about work?"

"You can help me finish it in my office tomorrow."

Let's hope I can convince him to let me try out a few fantasies on him instead.

CHAPTER 24

ETHAN

I roll over to find Addison still asleep next to me. Everything about this feels right. Having her in bed with me, waking up next to her; it seems like a dream. This is what I want in my life. I want *her* in my life, and I want to know everything about her—the good and bad. I don't want my life to be only about work anymore. I smile as she turns and curls into me, resting her head on my naked chest.

I know she's awake by the way she's breathing, but she doesn't open her eyes to look at me. "Addy, I need to get home so I can get ready for work." I run my fingers through her dark tresses, and she hums in appreciation.

"Or we can call in sick and spend the day together instead. Doesn't that sound like more fun?" She finally looks up at me, her chin resting on her hand over my chest.

Yes, that does sound very tempting. Images of the two of us getting to go out like a normal couple cross my mind, and I shake them away. I have too much to do at the office today, I need to be there.

"I can't. I have some meetings I can't push." I kiss her

quickly on the lips. "How about I pick you up a coffee this morning and we'll meet at the office?"

She sits up with a large smile on her face. "The big, bad Mr. Freeman is going to get *me* coffee for a change? What is the world coming to?" she teases.

She tries to get up, and I wrap my arms around her waist, pulling her back to me. "I didn't say I was done with you yet."

SHE'S ALREADY AT HER DESK WHEN I STROLL IN A LITTLE PAST nine a.m. She glances at me, her face blushing a bit when she meets my dark eyes. *I'd love to pull her into my office and fuck her against my desk.* I'm insatiable around her. Like she can read my thoughts, she gives a small shake of her head before focusing her gaze on the coffee in my hand.

I place a cup on her desk, and she looks up, raising an eyebrow at me. "Looks like you've got an admirer." I scrunch my face in confusion. She spins the cup to show me the number scribbled across the cream paper cup. "Wendy wants you to call her. Should I get her on the phone for you?"

She picks up the receiver, and I place my finger over the switch hook, silencing the dial tone. "If I wanted to set up a date, I would have done it there," I say. "You're the only one I want to date, Addy." She smiles warmly at me, a sparkle of delight in her eyes.

I check my calendar again for my next meeting, and it looks like I finally have some time to catch a breather. Addy strolls into my office in her blue pencil skirt, white blouse, and black high heels. Her hair is pulled back into a loose hairdo, and she has on just a splash of makeup. *Fucking beautiful... and all mine.*

I haven't told her yet, but I got HR to change the rules about no interoffice relationships. As long as the relationship doesn't interfere with work, there should be no issues. I know she has been worried about that, too, and I want to put her mind at ease.

She walks around my desk, and I push back in my chair, giving her room to stand between my legs as she leans against the heavy desk. "According to your calendar, you have a bit of free time," she coos.

God, I hope this is going where I think it is. "Hmmm, it appears I do."

She puts her hand on my chest and slides it all the way down until her nimble fingers rest over my crotch. She then slides the rest of her body down to the floor until she's kneeling at my feet. Her big green eyes dance with excitement as she pops the button on my pants and pulls down the zipper.

She reaches her hand in and pulls out my hardening cock. "Mmm, good girl," I purr as she wraps her fingers around the base and starts stroking up and down. Her lips meet the tip, and I thrust my hips up, seeking more of her warm mouth. *Shit, she feels perfect.* She works me over with an expert touch.

My body tenses as I think about that. She's very good at this, and I know she has had sex with clients at the strip club. My innocent Addison isn't innocent at all, and I start to pull away when my office door swings open unexpectedly. I scoot the chair in, pressing her further under my desk, shielding her from my father's dark, seedy eyes.

"You told him *no?*" he booms, his body shaking in anger. Addison stills in her movements, but my cock is still effectively down her throat. She takes a few deep breaths but holds still as I place my hands on the desk, leaning forward.

"We don't need to get involved with him. We have more than enough clients right now to keep the business successful. If you remember correctly, that's what I told the board this past weekend."

She starts bobbing her head up and down achingly slow, and it takes all of my strength to not groan in pleasure.

"You're making a big mistake, boy. The board already wants you gone. This is going to be the thing that pushes them over. I've fought for you because you're my son, but you're a fucking idiot walking away from Mr. Costanza a *second* time." He leans over my desk, and I slide in a little more, making sure to keep Addison completely hidden from view. "His business is just as good as any other client you've taken on, and he holds a lot of power. He can make this company."

He sizes me up and down, waiting for my reply. "I've already done that, Dad. After you got caught fucking your assistant and had a lot of bad press follow you, I had to work my ass off to prove we were the best in the business and not some HR nightmare." I give a snarky scoff. "I'm *still* cleaning up your fucking mess." *I wish Addy wasn't under the desk with her lips wrapped around me. I need the upper hand.* As if she can read my mind, she discreetly tucks me back into my pants, buttons me back up, and presses herself against the side of the desk. I rise, placing my hands on my desk, and level him with a stare. "Get the fuck out of my office before I have you arrested for trespassing."

"Watch out, Ethan. He's not someone you want to piss off." He turns and stalks out of the room before I can get another word out.

Addison crawls out from under my desk and looks up at me, still on her knees. She bites her lip, looking like she wants to say something, but doesn't. I sit back as she rubs up and down my inner thighs, soothing the tense muscles in my legs. That man makes me so Goddamn angry.

"Are you sure you're making the right decision?" she asks after a minute or two of silence.

"I know I am. We don't need Costanza, and if my father is

pushing for it, well, all the more reason *not* to take his business. The proposal he sent was fine. Some parts of it seemed a bit odd, but nothing we couldn't handle as far as a security assessment goes."

"But...?" she drags out the word.

"I get a bad feeling about him, and I don't want to get caught in the middle of something that could have been avoided." I lay my hand on the side of her face and run my finger up and down her cheek, soothing her. Her eyelids flutter closed as she takes a deep, calming breath. "Now, I think we were in the middle of finishing out one of the dirtiest fantasies I've ever had about you."

She opens her eyes and looks up at me, a smile gracing her lips. "You too, huh?"

I chuckle and shake my head. "You're something else, you know that?"

"Mmm, I know. And I'll let you in on a little secret." I lean over as she stretches so she can get close to my ear. "I've had way dirtier fantasies about you and this office than just a little blow job." My dick hardens again at her confession. "My favorite one to visit on lonely nights is you fucking me against the large window, fully on display so everyone down below can see."

She pulls me out of my pants and starts working me over again as the images she placed in my head bring my orgasm to the surface once more. *Addison, bare naked in front of me as I pound into her from behind, pressing her body against the cool glass. Her moans of pleasure edging me on until finally...*

"Fuck," I groan, pumping my hips up and down into her mouth. She greedily takes me down her throat and moans around my length. "Good girl, I'm going to come. Swallow everything." She gives a subtle nod of her head and sucks harder so as to not lose a drop. I hold her head down over me as I thrust up one more time, spilling down the back of her throat. My heart is beating frantically as she licks and sucks me clean. She smiles up at me from the floor, and I can't help the overwhelming feeling that I'm falling in *love* with this naughty girl.

How is that even possible?

CHAPTER 25

ADDISON

The girls are hanging on my bed as I pack for my long weekend trip to Virginia with Ethan. The wine is flowing as we gossip about life and the club. Eden sits in silence, listening with a small smile on her face. I know she's happy for us, but I really want her to find someone who loves her for the badass she is. She deserves it after all the shit she's gone through in her life.

Nights like these are becoming few and far between now that two of the girls have settled down and started families. I miss this, though. Getting to spend time laughing with my girls makes everything right with the world. I asked them to come over tonight while I pack because I'm nervous about my weekend, and they dropped everything for me. They are the best friends a girl could ever have, and I'm so thankful for them.

My aunt and uncle are still around, so I do have *some* family I can turn to, but these girls are my rocks. *They are my true family.* I swipe at a stray tear that's threatening to fall and give them a big smile before taking a sip of my wine.

"Addy, what's gotten into you tonight? Are you on your period?" Everleigh gasps, "Are you pregnant?"

I roll my eyes at Everleigh's questions and give them a big sigh. "No to both, bitch. I'm nervous about bringing him home to," I make air quotes, "meet the family. I've never brought anyone back with me, not even you girls, and I'm worried that him seeing this will change what's happening. We have a good thing going right now, and I've wanted him for so damn long."

Every year, Eden asks if I want company, and I give her a sad smile and tell her I'll be okay on my own. Lia and Everleigh stopped asking after a few years of me turning them down, but I know they would jump if I asked.

I put fresh flowers at each of my family member's graves, tell them about my life and how things are going with the club and with my job, and I cry. A lot. No one needs to see that.

There have been some years that are harder than others, but I always find strength when visiting and talking with them. Once the weekend is over, I usually have a clearer head and come back ready to face whatever the world throws at me.

Lia chimes in, "Addy, that can't be the only thing weighin' on your mind. He already knows about your family and your past—"

I shake my head sadly. "No. He doesn't know everything. He doesn't know what happened between me and his dad, or his ties with Vince. It was when we were at *The Devil's Playground*, but still." I fold and unfold the shirt in my hands, trying to distract myself. "He also doesn't know about my... promiscuity. Some of the men are even people that I work with now." *God, I really am a slut.*

As if the girls can hear my inner thoughts, they chuckle. "Never thought you'd want to give up your boy toys because someone finally won you over," Everleigh jokes.

I chuckle, but it's not sincere. For once in my life, I'm

ashamed of the choices I've made. I'm ashamed that I grabbed my sexuality by the horns and ran with it because if my maneater ways come out, it could ruin the one good thing I have going—besides my girls, that is.

"Relationships are built on trust. You need to open up to him at some point and tell him what's going on. He's earned your history, your demons," Eden adds.

My phone pings, and I look down at the text from Ethan.

Ethan: *Are you sure I can't convince you to sleep here tonight? I'm sure we could explore more of those fantasies you have yet to tell me about.*

I roll my eyes but can't help the smile that graces my lips. For the first time in a *long* time, I'm truly happy. I'm not just rolling with the punches; I'm actually experiencing life. My heart constricts at the thought of losing him.

No.

He will never know about my past at The Devil's Playground... it would kill him.

He doesn't need to know what I did to make it through those tough times or how Vince tried to break me down. Hell, even I don't need to remember those times. Yes, they got me to where I need to be, but it's my cross to bear, no one else's.

Me: *Sorry, lover boy, I have a hot date here tonight.*

"Smile, girls," I say and snap a picture before I send it off to him.

I'm not ignoring Eden's comment, although from the shrug she's giving me, I'm sure she feels like I am. But the past is the past. I'm not ready to tell it. There is nothing I can do to change it, and she knows that. It's how I became the person I am today, and without it, who knows where I would be.

Probably buried six feet under.

The thought sends a shiver down my spine, and I rub the faded scar on my left wrist absentmindedly.

"We're supposed to be having fun tonight, so stop looking like someone kicked your puppy. Finish packing and then we can pop in a movie," Everleigh chimes in, taking my wrist in her hand to stop the movement.

I shake my head to rid the dark thoughts that are there. She's right. Tonight is for happy memories, not memories I'd rather forget.

I SLIDE INTO ETHAN'S CAR, AND HE HANDS ME A PAPER CUP OF coffee. I take a sip of the warm drink and close my eyes, gripping the cup between my hands. *Heaven.* As he places his hand on my thigh, I look over at him, and he pulls out onto the road to the freeway to take us to the airport.

"Morning, beautiful," he says.

A contented sigh leaves my lips. "Good morning, handsome."

"Sleep well?"

Not particularly. I tossed and turned for a lot of the night, worried that something was going to go wrong or that he would decide he didn't want to come after all. I shouldn't be this worried about showing him *this* part of my life. This part isn't as messy as other parts, but it doesn't make it easier.

Ethan is getting a piece of me no one else ever has. That's a big step.

"Fine, just nervous for the trip. You?"

He rubs circles on my thigh, and I scoot down lower,

sinking into the expensive leather seats. "There's nothing to be nervous about. If I didn't want to be here, I wouldn't be. I want to see this part of you—the life you had to leave behind. Maybe it will help me understand a bit more about you and some of the secrets you keep."

All my muscles go rigid. *What does he mean by that? What does he know that he's not telling me?* I start running through any and all conversations I've had with him, or the ones I can remember anyway. Was there something I've said to make him feel I'm keeping secrets?

Well, you are, dummy.

My entire adult life has been one secret to the next. The lines of truth get blurred from time to time, and there have been moments I've gotten lost in what is real and what's fake. I take a sip of my coffee to distract myself. This is not how I anticipated the drive to the airport would be. He's trusted me with some of his secrets and has let me into his life.

Shouldn't I be willing to do the same for him?

Addison has barely said two words to me since we left her apartment. I figured it was nerves and that by the time we landed she would be telling me about her hometown, but the most I've gotten out of her is an address to a flower shop.

I glance at her, but she's looking out the passenger window, ignoring me—pulling away. I knew this would be hard for her, especially when I sprung the idea on her, but she can't shut me out.

"Addy, will you tell me what you're thinking?" I ask, breaking the silence.

"Nothing," she replies instantly.

"Please, babe. It's not nothing. Are you thinking about your family?" I reach over the console to stroke her leg, anything to get her to open up to me.

"Yes." She doesn't offer me anything else for a few minutes but then opens up again. "You know my past isn't the greatest, right? It was until my family died, but after that, things went downhill."

I don't know much about her past, but this is a start. "I

know you worked at the strip club, and probably had to do some things you aren't proud of. It's the past, though. I'm willing to look past what you had to do to survive. You're not in the same place you were all those years ago. You've grown up, changed." I glance between her and the road, looking for any type of acknowledgment. "You shouldn't be so hard on yourself. You did what you had to."

"What if I've done some things I didn't have to but *wanted* to?" It comes out so quiet, I almost don't catch it all.

"We all make mistakes, Addy. No one's perfect." I continue rubbing soothing circles on her leg.

She nods but goes back to looking out the window as we pass through a small town. "Up here on your left," she says, pointing to a small row of shops. I pull into an empty spot, and we walk into the flower shop. The bell above the door rings, and an elderly woman smiles warmly at us.

"Addison, your call surprised me. Isn't it a bit early for you to come for a visit?"

"Hi, Mrs. Dickerson. Yeah, a change of plans this year." She takes my hand in hers and gives me a warm smile, the first one I've seen from her today.

"Oh, and who is this handsome man?" The elderly woman smiles at Addy and extends her hand for me.

"I'm Ethan Freeman, her boyfriend." It dawns on me as I say it, we haven't formally discussed labels. I glance at her from the corner of my eye, but she doesn't seem taken aback by my response. Instead, her smile widens. *Guess she likes the idea as much as I do.*

The woman gasps as her smile spreads wider. "Well, it's nice to meet you, dear. I'm glad to see Addison has found herself a nice man." She looks between us one more time and heads to the fridge to pull out three floral arrangements. She places them on the counter, and Addy leans down, smelling the irises.

I hand the woman my card to pay for them, and Addy opens her mouth to argue. I place my finger over her lips and give her a warm smile. "Let me take care of this for you." She swallows thickly and nods her head.

We get back into the car, and she gives me directions to the cemetery next. When we pull up along the set of three gravestones, she takes a shuddering breath before pushing open the car door. I've known this woman professionally for a few years, and she has never once shown her emotions like they are on display right now.

She looks back at me when I make no move to get out. I know this was a hard decision for her to make, allowing me to come. "Do you mind waiting for a few minutes?"

"I'll be here if you need me."

She nods and closes the door. I watch her place the flowers by the three graves and remove some weeds from around the gravesite. She kneels on the green grass, talking quietly to them. I wonder if she tells them about her life and what has been going on. How many of her secrets has she confided in these heavy pieces of marble? Do they know them all or does she hide from them as well?

She drops her head to her chest, and her body shakes. *Shit.* I step out and wrap my arms around her, pulling her against my chest. Her sobs rip through the quiet surrounding us, exposing the tremendous turmoil she keeps bottled up. My girl is so brave in front of everyone, but here... here, she can be herself. She can let all the hurt and frustration go.

I rub the back of her head and sway gently, whispering soothing words in her ear, wishing I could take her pain away. I would do anything to take this pain from her and make it my own. She grips me tightly, pulling me even closer to her as her tears stain the front of my shirt. The way her body ripples under my grasp displays the true agony she feels at being here.

After a few more minutes, I ask, "Want to tell me about it?" She shakes her head and takes a deep breath, burying her face in my neck and holding on to me as if I'm her lifeline.

"Shh, baby girl, it's okay." I stroke her back. Slowly, her body relaxes in my embrace. She takes one more deep breath before looking up into my face. Her green eyes are bright with tears, and I swipe under her eyes, removing some mascara. Her face is a little puffy from all the crying, but even still, she's the most beautiful woman I've ever laid eyes on.

She pulls away to wipe her own face, saying with a chuckle, "God, I'm such a hot mess," trying to play it off as a joke.

"Addison, don't." She tilts her head and furrows her brows in confusion. "Don't act like you shouldn't be upset by this. This is your family—your mom, dad, and brother. Don't push this pain down. Get it out. I'll be here for you, however you need me, or I can leave you alone for a bit."

My heart races when she looks like she's going to cry again. *Maybe that wasn't the best thing to tell her. Is this when she pushes me away?*

"We got into a big fight. I stormed out of the house to go visit my boyfriend." The tears start falling down her face again as she looks up to the blue sky, blinking the water away. "I told my mom I hated her." She chuckles, but it's full of malice. "I was *mad* at her because she wouldn't buy me a pair of boots I saw at the store that I loved. They were too expensive. *How selfish is that?*"

I take her hands in mine, rubbing the backs of them, urging her to continue. "It's not selfish. You were a teenager. I have two sisters, remember?" I point out. "You loved her. She knew that."

"She was always buying Oliver, my brother, stuff for soccer, and I felt like I never got anything I wanted." She turns to look at her mom's headstone. "I know it's not true. She bought me almost everything I asked for." She turns to look at me again, a fresh wave of tears streaming down her face. "I cooled down and was ready to apologize, but as I turned down the street, I saw the fire and all the trucks surrounding the house.

"I pushed through a few of the firemen, rushing into the house to look for them, but I couldn't get to them. There was too much smoke. Someone rushed in after me and carried me out, back to safety. If I didn't get mad at her, I would have died with them that day. I would have been with my family. It would have been tragic, but I wouldn't have to live with this *guilt* every fucking day." Her voice cracks as more tears fall down her face.

I pull her to me, hugging her as tight as I possibly can, trying to take away some of the guilt and burden she has put on herself. Addison Snyder is one of the strongest women I have ever met. I don't think I would have survived the shit she went through and still come out on top. She's a fighter and should be damn proud of where she is in her life—no matter the way she got here.

"Thank you," I whisper into her hair before I kiss her head. "Thank you for sharing your family with me."

"Ethan, can we go to the room for a little bit?"

She must be exhausted from the emotional rollercoaster she's been on since we got here. I couldn't deny this girl anything right now, even if I wanted to. I help her stand and get into the car.

"You told Mrs. Dickerson you were my boyfriend. Is that how you see us?"

No point in lying to her, not after the hell she's just gone through. "Yeah, Addy, I do."

"I have a lot of scars," she warns.

I may not know the full extent of her scars and what she has been hiding, but there is no denying she's it for me. I feel her the moment she enters the room without even having to look up. It's as if my body knows who it wants and has attuned itself to her. I'm willing to fight her demons with her, and together, we will get through anything.

"Scars make the most interesting stories."

CHAPTER 27

ADDISON

I open my eyes to find Ethan sitting next to me, his laptop open, typing away. *You can take him away from work, but you can't actually make him stop working.* I shift my weight and snuggle in closer to his warmth. Usually, when I visit my family, I have a hard time sleeping after, but today was... different.

Ethan being here has taken some of the burden from my shoulders.

When we got to the room, we laid down in bed, and I cried more as he held me and whispered soothing words in my ear and rubbed my back until I finally dozed off.

"Hey," my voice croaks from all the crying and lack of use.

He looks down at me and smiles before moving his computer to the table and snuggling down next to me again, wrapping his arms around me. "Hey, beautiful, feel better?" He pushes some loose hair away from my face and kisses the tip of my nose.

"Much." I try to sit up, but he holds me in place, rubbing up and down my back.

"I made us dinner plans if you're up for it, and then I thought we could catch a movie or something."

I titter. "The big CEO Ethan Freeman can make his own dinner plans? I better watch out, or I'll be out of a job."

He snorts and shakes his head before burying his nose in my hair, inhaling deeply. "You can't get away from me that easily. Besides, I've never had an assistant as *in tune* with my needs as you are, Ms. Snyder." He licks his lower lip, and his eyes darken.

His cock twitches in his pants, and when I reach my hand down to feel him, he takes my wrist in his. He gives me a subtle shake of his head and rolls me to my back. I instinctually spread my thighs, inviting him in. *Needing him.*

"Please, Ethan," I beg as I lift my hips to him. "I need you."

He dips his head to my neck, peppering kisses along my collarbone and fluttering pulse. He makes me feel so good, so *alive.* I've always used men to make me feel something—anything. Nothing I have experienced has come close to this, though. The way he infiltrates my mind, body, and soul is unnerving.

He grinds down into me but pulls away as I reach down for him. I growl in frustration. His breath fans across my heated skin before his lips skim the outer shell of my ear. "You've had an emotional day and need to eat something first." He presses down one last time for good measure, then climbs off me.

"Where are we going for dinner?"

He helps me stand, and I find my way to the bathroom.

"It's an Italian place in the next town over, *Bella E Buona.* It has good reviews."

I pop my head out to look at him. "Yeah, it has good reviews because it's almost impossible to get a reservation. That place opened about three years ago, and the wait was almost two months long before they even opened their doors."

"Have you ever been?" He's still sitting on the bed, waiting for me to come back into the room. I flip off the light and saunter back to him. I kneel on the edge of the bed and slowly crawl my way up to him, between his legs. My eyes never leave his big brown ones.

I cage him in, my hands on either side of his waist and my face inches from his. "Yes."

I expect him to lean up and try to kiss me, or say some sort of sexual innuendo, but he doesn't. Instead, he reaches his hands out to my sides and starts tickling me. I jerk away and shriek in surprise, trying to get away from his roaming hands. He's too big, though, and pins me easily to the bed, his hands never stopping.

I buck up like a wild horse, laughing and screaming as his fingers dig into my sides and under my arms. "Looks like someone's ticklish," he taunts.

"Uncle!" I scream, trying to catch my breath. "Uncle," I repeat as his attack slows down. He keeps me pinned under his weight, a huge grin spread across his face. My laughter comes out in short bursts until it finally stops, and then I lay still under him.

"I like the way you laugh, Addy. I wish I could hear it more often." He leans down to kiss my lips. His are soft and gentle against mine, and when I lean up for more, he pulls back.

"I laugh," I retort defensively.

His smile is sad. "Yeah, but not like this. You laugh like you have the world on your shoulders and are just trying to stay afloat."

You have no idea, Ethan. I slide off the bed, gathering my bag so we can head out. I don't say anything else, and he doesn't push the subject. I'm thankful for the silence surrounding us as we get into the rental car to leave for dinner. My rumbling stomach fills the quiet space between us and I rub it.

Ethan opens his mouth to say something and closes it again as we pull into a parking space. The restaurant is just like I remember it, small but elegant looking. It's a nice change of pace from the small coffee shops that litter most of the surrounding towns.

The hostess seats us toward the back, and Ethan holds my chair out like a true gentleman. Once we're settled and order a drink, I start talking again.

"I've never brought anyone home with me—not even the girls. Thank you for doing this. It was nice not being alone today, especially when I feel like I drown in loneliness." I want to tell him really just how fucked up I am. How I use men to feel *anything*. Used. I haven't slept with anyone except Ethan since he came into the club.

"I'm sorry."

"You're who made me want to get my MBA. Did you know that?" He shakes his head, a smile spreading across his face. I shrug. "Of course, you wouldn't, I've never told you. It was after we met for the first time at the club. You gave me hope."

"How did I do that?"

"You didn't hurt me that night. You asked instead of just taking. You were my beacon of light in an otherwise dim situation." His smile fades. *Shit. Backpedal, Addison.* "You were young and successful."

"Ah, yes, nepotism at its finest. Thanks, Dad." He takes a sip of his drink and continues. "Don't get me wrong, I had to put in the work to get my degree, but the chances of me becoming CEO this young were be slim unless I started my own company." I bite my lip, trying to decide if he's mad or not. "You, though, Addy, you figured it out all on your own. You worked your ass off to get to where you are today."

I feel a blush creep up my neck and settle into my cheeks.

It's not often one receives praise from the CEO of the company. How the hell am I going to tell him I basically stalked him from the moment he left cash on the table after we had sex without sounding like a crazy psycho?

Maybe I need to give it more time before I share *all* the skeletons in my closet.

I'M SO GLAD ETHAN CAME WITH ME THIS WEEKEND, I DIDN'T know how much I needed him there with me, or how much I wanted to show him that side of me. I step into my apartment building, and Shane, the doorman, holds out an envelope for me.

"Good afternoon, Ms. Snyder. This was dropped off for you this weekend."

I smile warmly at him and tuck it under my arm with a thanks. I look at the writing. In black Sharpie, it has my name scrawled across it, but no other identifying information or a return address. *Strange.*

When I get into my apartment, I drop my overnight bag off and rip open the envelope, pulling the documents out. The first image I see makes me drop the whole thing to the ground and cover my mouth.

My house, on fire. It's a black and white photo, but I would recognize the colonial anywhere. I squeeze my eyes shut and take a deep breath before I pick everything back up. My heart is beating so hard I feel as if I've just run a marathon.

I put the stack on the table and start shuffling through all the contents. There are multiple pictures of my family, out in public. They all look like something a private investigator would have. Clearly, we were unaware these were taken. There are a few of Oliver and my mom, but most of them were of me and my dad.

Next is some financial paperwork. Deposits and withdrawals from one account to another. My dad's name is at the top, but I'm not familiar with this bank, and there are a lot of big withdrawals made. What the hell was he up to?

I try to think. Dad used to take trips to visit Atlanta for work. One of the subsidiaries was down this way for the company he worked for, and he always paid a visit to Aunt Linda, his sister. He would travel every few months. On occasion, it would be a family trip, and all of us would come. He would go to a few meetings during the day, sometimes the evening, and then we would spend time together.

"Dad, what were you caught up in?" I ask myself.

Next is the report on the fire. I remember seeing the report from the police, and it was an accident—a spark from a faulty outlet, that's what it said. But this... this report isn't the one I saw. It's dated correctly, but this shows the cause of the fire was arson. My hands shake as I read the words on the paper again.

Arson.

I sink into the chair next to me and stare at the five-letter word. Someone deliberately set fire to my house, killed my parents and brother. Why? Were they trying to kill us all? It wasn't that late at night, so surely, someone who would want to kill all of us would have known I wasn't home, especially if they had been watching.

Which means this was deliberate. Keeping me alive was the plan all along.

There's one picture behind the report, a picture of my dad shaking hands with Vince Perelli.

I open a new text to the girls.

Me: *I need you girls here, now. Ev, bring Kieran and your dad.*

Everleigh: *What's wrong?*

Me: *Just get here ASAP.*

Eden knocks on my door almost immediately, using her spare key when I don't open it fast enough. She stands in the doorway and stares at me, waiting for me to speak.

"My dad knew Vince, and the fire wasn't an accident. It was arson."

"Is there anything you can uncover about why Vince had my house destroyed?"

Mr. Greene shakes his head, a grim look on his face. "This is over ten years old. Unless we had records from Vince, there's really no way of knowing what was going on."

I look around the room at my friends, and everyone looks at me with sorrow. *How the hell did this happen?*

I wrap my arms around myself, wishing Ethan was here. "Was me coming here all part of a master plan he had? Meeting you all?" I ask more to myself than anyone.

"Vince was a bastard, but I honestly don't know." Eden reaches out to touch my arm, and I pull back from her a bit.

"I'll see if I can find anything, maybe make a few phone calls up to Virginia. In the meantime, don't mention this to anyone. You need to keep this to yourself, Addison," Kieran warns.

I nod in understanding. "Okay."

I hand the documents over to Kieran and hesitate before letting go. "Addy…"

"Don't fuck me over, Kieran. I need these answers if you can get them."

He nods as I give him all the documents. "I'll try to get some answers for you."

CHAPTER 28

ETHAN

The rest of the weekend went by too quickly. It was nice to get away, but with the new projects we are working on, I still felt like I was at work. Addison seems happier by the time we get home though, and the thought that I had a helping hand in that, makes me smile.

She steps into my office, puts a coffee down on my desk, and sits in the chair opposite of me. My gaze lands on her heel-clad foot and slowly travels up the length of her body, admiring her strong legs and slim waist. My gaze travels higher until I'm admiring her beautiful face.

She pops an eyebrow at me. "See anything you like, Mr. Freeman?"

"Everything," I all but growl.

She pushes her legs apart enough for me to see up her skirt and notice she has no panties on under her fitted dress. *God damn this woman is going to kill me.* I lick my lips and hum deep in my throat in appreciation.

"Lia and Landry are having a cookout this weekend and

invited the girls and their men. I hoped you'd come with me so I can show you off."

"Sure, sounds fun. I'd like to be able to spend more time with your friends, get to know them." *Maybe try to uncover some of the mystery that still surrounds you.*

Addison's opened up to me so much since our visit to Virginia, but I still feel like she's hiding something from me. I know I said her past is her past, and I meant it; I just wish she felt comfortable enough to tell me about it. Maybe I can help her sort through what's bothering her. Remind her she's not that same girl anymore.

"Great, I'll pick you up at one on Saturday so we can head over together. It'll be nice to get together with everyone. It doesn't happen as much now that Lia and Everleigh are married with kids." She stands and smooths the skirt of her dress out.

She heads for the door, and I stand, leaning over my desk. "Lock the door, Addy." She takes a shuddering breath and does as I ask. She stands there, chin tucked toward her chest, waiting for my next command. "You can't come in here with no panties on and not expect to get fucked over my desk."

She smirks as she turns to me. "Guess my master plan is working then." She saunters over to my desk and stands in front of me, dragging her finger down my chest. I hiss when she stops at the bulge in my pants and gives a little squeeze. "Always so hard for me, Ethan."

She turns, places her hands on my desk, and presses her chest down. God, seeing her in this position is a wet dream. She's so fucking sexy, and she's all mine. After our trip to Virginia, things between us have been even hotter, if that's possible. Neither of us can keep our hands off each other. She's even started sleeping at my place fairly regularly.

With the exception of last night. She had a shift at *RISE* and told me she had to go. I understand it's her other job, and I understand she is part owner, but I don't want anyone else looking at or touching her. She doesn't need to be dancing for other men. I know it's more than that for her, but it's still a hard pill to swallow.

I'm sure that's what some of this is all about. She's trying to make it up to me because I all but begged her not to go. She promised it would be a slow night and said she only had one set, but she also needed to check on the books and do some paperwork. It took everything in me not to drive my ass down there to make sure no one was giving her problems.

Instead, I teased her all night by sending her dirty text messages, hoping to drive her insane so she would come back home where I could give her a fucking like no one else can. I missed having her in my bed when I woke up this morning. I've gotten used to being curled around her, so my big bed felt cold and empty.

She looks over her shoulder as she pulls the bottom of her dress up over her hips, her pretty pinky pussy and ass on full display for me. "Please, Ethan," she moans, adjusting her stance to allow me between her legs.

I pull the zipper down on my pants, the teeth seemingly echoing off the walls in anticipation. Then I push my pants down past my hips and stroke my cock, moving it up and down the slit of her ass. I know we have to be quiet, but I want to smack her ass so red she feels it long after I've stopped.

"Are you going to let me fill you up like a good girl?" I ask, teasing her with the head of my cock.

"Mmm," she hums, gasping when I squeeze her ass hard in my hand, then pull her cheeks apart, only to be met with a surprise. She has a pretty pink butt plug nestled between her cheeks.

"Addy, what's this?" I ask, tapping the jewel.

She moans. "A present for you."

"You're keeping that in the rest of the day, and I'm taking your ass tonight." I pull her dress down over her hips and help her stand.

The shocked look on her face is worth the case of blue balls I'll have the rest of the day in anticipation for tonight.

"No sex?"

I shrug. "Shouldn't have come in here with a plug in your ass."

The utter look of shock on her face has me stifling a laugh. Then she narrows her eyes and saunters out of my office with extra sway to her hips. She is full of surprises. Anytime I think I have her figured out, she throws a curveball at me.

ADDISON DIDN'T WAIT FOR ME TO LEAVE TONIGHT. SHE TAKES off before me, and if she's smart, she's heading over to my place. I gave her a key to let herself in and already called Rhonda to take the night off. I don't want any interruptions. I order some take-out I can pick up on the way so I can at least make sure she eats.

As I go to step out my office door, dear old Dad steps through the front door, holding a manila envelope in his hand. He holds it out to me without saying a word as he stalks toward me.

"What the hell's in there?" I ask without taking the information from him when he stops in front of me.

"Something you might want to have a look at."

"If this is about working with Al, I told you, it's not happening. We even had a vote by the board, and if you remember correctly, they sided with me after we went over the other projects currently on the table." I hope he doesn't miss the air of smugness in my voice.

"I remember. This doesn't have anything to do with Al. Open it," he urges.

"I'm busy tonight. I'll do it later." I turn and toss it in a random drawer.

"You're not any better than me, Ethan. Open that and see what I mean."

CHAPTER 29

ADDISON

I stopped at my favorite toy shop before driving over to Ethan's tonight. I wanted to make tonight extra special. He was pissed off at me last night when I went to *RISE*, and if I'm honest, it's the first time I didn't have fun dancing. I wanted to be home, cuddled up with Ethan, even if it didn't lead to sex. *Not that we've ever had that problem.*

Home.

When is the last time any place has truly felt that way? My apartment is nice and all, but it's always just felt like a place to lay my head at night. I haven't truly felt like I've been home since the fire.

Even spending time with my girls, at the end of the night, I always came home alone, with no one to share my life with. And isn't that what we all want? Someone to share life with? To not feel forgotten in this crazy messed up world we're in? Ethan is that for me. He's my home. I don't have to pretend around him. I can just be myself.

I change out of the dress I wore today and shimmy into my new black and pink lingerie, complete with a mask. I pull the thigh-high stockings up my legs and step foot into my high black heels again. I fluff my curled hair around my shoulders and dab some lip gloss on my lips with my finger before puckering them out.

The plug in my ass has been driving me insane all day. I was even tempted to touch myself in the women's bathroom at the office. I was just about to when someone else walked in and I lost my nerve. Besides, the best orgasms always come from edging.

I flinch when the front door opens and slams against the back wall. *Shit, I wonder what has his panties in a twist?* I walk out into the living room as he puts a few bags of food on the table. He doesn't see me until I clear my throat.

"Jesus Christ," he mumbles as he digs his fingers through his hair.

"Addison Snyder, actually," I quip and smile warmly at him. "Is everything okay, Mr. Freeman?"

"It is now." He stalks toward me, and I keep my head held high as he digs his fingers into my hips. I hope he leaves marks. I love being able to feel him still on me the next day. He dips his head, pressing his lips against mine with such force it steals my breath from me. There is so much electricity behind it, it's almost frightening.

He walks me backward until we are in his room, then slams the door shut behind us. He spins me around and places my hands on the edge of the bed. I stay exactly where he put me as he walks around me, touching me. His fingers are mapping every curve of my body, raising goosebumps on my skin.

I offer him a breathy sigh as he continues his ministrations. His fingers slide to a stop on my left ass cheek, and he smacks it hard. I rear up and gasp in shock as he pushes me back down to the bed.

"That's for being a tease all damn day." He smacks my right

cheek just as hard, the sting sending a new wave of arousal through me, and I moan. "That's for keeping me hard all day, knowing you've been prepping your pretty little ass for me."

I hear the rustle of his clothing as he bends down behind me. I feel his breath on my lower back, but it's when his wet tongue darts out and licks around the pink plug that I think I might die.

"Oh God, Ethan." I push my hips back to him. His fingers grip the plug, and he starts playing with it, pulling it gently, but not with enough force to remove it. I drop my head and breathe through the torture. I'm never going to last with what he's doing to me.

"What a pretty little ass, Addy. I love knowing you've stuffed it full for me. Have you been wet all day?" He slides a finger through my slick heat, and I bite my lip, muffling a moan.

"Yes."

"Did you touch your pussy today, knowing I was going to fuck your ass tonight? Did you touch my pussy, Addy?"

I shake my head. "No. I wanted to, and I almost did, but someone walked into the bathroom."

He laughs darkly behind me and stands up. "Fuck, that's so Goddamn hot. I love knowing you would have touched yourself in the bathroom at work. Next time, I want you to, and you can send me a picture." He starts stripping out of his clothes. I turn my head in time for him to push his pants down his muscular legs. "Or better yet, come to my office and let me watch you. Some of my phone meetings are boring. I'd love to have a distraction." He smiles wide as he strokes his cock.

I reach forward on the bed and hand him a bottle of lube. He pulls the plug out with a pop and rubs the lube up and down his thick length. This isn't the first time I've had anal, but it hopefully will be the best time. I would never do this with clients at the club. I'm kinky and willing to do all sorts of stuff to make their fantasies come true, but not this.

He rubs the length of my back and massages some of the muscles that have bunched. "Are you sure about this?"

Instead of responding to him, I press my hips back and line his cock up with my puckered hole. He presses forward, slowly, allowing my body to open for him. There is a slight burn, but most of it slides easily from wearing the plug for so long.

"Shit, Addy. You're so fucking tight." He grabs my cheeks and spreads them to watch his cock slide all the way in. When I feel his balls pressed against my ass, I breathe deeply. I reach blindly for the other thing I bought at the shop today, a dildo.

"What's that for?" he asks, gripping my hips.

I sigh in pleasure. "Ever experienced double-penetration before?"

"Nope, and we aren't doing that tonight. If we're going to do that, I'm not claiming your ass for it. I'm gonna come deep in your pussy. Drop the dildo and fuck yourself on my cock."

Bossy. But I love when he's like this. I reach my hand down to stroke my clit, although I'm not even sure I need to in order to get off. Then I press back into him, fucking him how I want, taking what I need from him. My movements start off slow, but the pace quickly picks up. The sound of slapping skin echoes through the room as our heavy breathing mixes.

"You feel so fucking good, Addy. I want you to come and squeeze my cock," he groans out.

You don't have to tell me twice. I rub a few more tight circles over my bundle of nerves and go off like a rocket. He holds my hips as my movements become jerky, taking over control as I ride the waves of one of the most intense orgasms of my life.

I bite my fingers to keep from screaming, but he's not

having that. He grabs my hair and pulls my face away from the mattress as he pounds into me. He pants and thrusts hard a few more times before I feel his body tense behind me. He holds me flush against him and stills inside of me, his throbbing dick filling me up.

He brushes some hair away from my neck and kisses me gently. So unlike the animalistic behavior he just exhibited moments ago. Now, his touch is gentle. He's beginning to soften in me, and when he pulls out, we both groan at the loss.

"Let's shower and have dinner. I got food from *Gusto's*. Hope you like burgers. They have the best there." I wrap my arms around his waist and lay my head on his chest, listening to the steady rhythm of his heartbeat.

After this weekend, I'm going to tell him about everything. I just need a few more days before he might hate me. I'm not ready to give him back yet, not when Ethan Freeman is the best damn thing that's happened to me.

I hope, when I explain everything—how I started at the club, choosing my career path with the intention of working for him, and everything with his dad, that he'll understand I didn't have a choice for some of my actions.

CHAPTER 30

ETHAN

I can't get Addison out of my damn head. She surprises me at every turn. Just when I think I've figured her out, she does something like a few nights ago with the sex toys. Fuck, it was so hot.

I love her. There is no doubt in my mind that she's the girl for me. I need to get over my issues with her working at the club. Lia still works there from time to time, and it seems Landry is fine with it. Maybe there are some special perks to her working there...

My phone buzzes with a new message from Landry. Speak of the devil.

Landry: *Heard you're coming to the cookout tomorrow. It'll be good to not be as overrun by the female population.*

Me: *Watch it, I'll have Addy tell Lia what you said and you'll be in the dog house until next year.*

Landry: *I'm sure she could kick my ass easily with all the kickboxing classes she does. I'm surprised Addy hasn't shown you a few moves.*

Me: *She's shown me a few moves all right. Just not the self-defense kind.*

Speak of the devil. Addison knocks on the door and smiles warmly at me. "Hey, I'm going to head out a bit early. I have a few errands to run, and then I have to go to the club. One of the girls called out, and I said I'd cover her shift."

My smile pulls down into a frown at the mention of her doing another shift there. I don't want her putting on a show for other men. She's *mine.*

"Please don't, Addy. You don't need to work there anymore." She opens her mouth to say something, and I hold my hand up, stopping her. I stand from behind my desk and walk over to her, closing the door behind us. No need for everyone to know her little secret. "I don't like you being there. It's not safe, and I don't want you taking your clothes off for anyone else."

She crosses her arms over her chest and pushes her hip out to the side. "You done?" she sasses.

I shake my head. "No. Besides the fact you co-own the place, why do you still need to dance?" *No time like the present to get this out in the open.*

She tosses her arms up and slams them back down over her hips. "Where's this coming from, Ethan? You know the men there don't mean anything to me. I share the stage time with some of the other girls, especially if one can't come in for whatever reason, like tonight. Plus, I enjoy dancing. I've been doing it since *long* before you knew I existed or cared."

My jaw ticks and I take a deep breath before I start talking. I keep my voice low and under control, even though I want to scream at her. "Because you're better than that girl. You told me you started stripping to get by, but you don't need to anymore. You have a good job, with good pay. Fuck, Addy, do you want to me increase your salary? Would that make it better?"

She narrows her eyes at me, her entire face turning red in anger. "Screw you, Ethan. Don't judge my choices when you don't understand my reasons. You know it's not about the money, and don't make me out like a whore."

"Isn't that basically what you were the night we fucked nine years ago?" Her hand comes at my face so fast I don't have time to respond as the sting behind her slap burns my cheek. The sound echoes in the quiet office. I keep my focus on the floor next to me. I deserved that.

I know I need time to get my head on straight, and if I try to talk to her right now, it's not going to end well. "Go," I command. She doesn't even glance back as she opens the door and gathers her stuff. I watch her retreating form as she walks through the office front door and gets into the elevator, not even sparing me a glance.

How the fuck do I keep managing to put my foot in my damn mouth? I open the top drawer of my desk and see the envelope my dad handed me earlier this week. Now's as good a time as ever. I know if I try to focus on work right now, I won't be able to concentrate. At least, this way, I can see what the old man is up to.

I pull a bunch of papers out, and a few photos fall out onto the desk. I look at the pictures first and turn my face up in repulsion. *Who the fuck managed to get these?* There are several of me and Ember, from the first night we were together. It's not possible that these should even exist. I have her pressed against the wall, I'm shoved deep inside her, and the look of her face is pure bliss.

There is another one of me fingering her while my face is buried in her neck, but there's no denying it's me. Again, her face is twisted in pure ecstasy in the picture. She has on a mask, but I would remember this night anywhere.

The next set of pictures, though, I think I really will be sick. Addy is straddling my father. I'd know her body anywhere. His pants are down around his thighs, and his hands are on her hips, holding her in place. Addison... *my Addison...* slept with my father and didn't even bother to tell me.

Maybe she didn't know it was him? My mind is spinning as I try to make heads or tails of what I'm looking at. I flip through a few more pictures, all of them different men and all of them with *the same girl.* I knew she slept with people, but I assumed it was a once in a while thing, not all the time.

I drop the pictures. My whole body feels numb, but with shaky hands, I pick up the small stack of papers. There are several pages filled with names, dates, and times. Addison's name is at the top of the paper, and the words *The Devil's Playground* is printed on the letterhead. There must be over a hundred names here, some of them repeat customers.

She did what she had to do to get by.

I stop at the last name on the page in my hand. *Ethan Freeman.* I turn the sheet of paper over, expecting to see more, but there aren't any. *The old man must have stopped at my name to make a point.* Have I always been the endgame for her? Was this all part of some big scheme to drag my name through the mud and ruin the reputation of the company? *To ruin me?*

I Google some of the names to see the type of men she slept with, the type of men she let *touch her.* Image after image infiltrates my mind as I continue the search. Young, old, skinny, fat, it doesn't matter. If they were willing to pay, she was willing to sleep with them. It doesn't appear she had a preference. As long as the money is good... who cares.

I pick up my phone and dial *his* number. He picks up after a few rings with a smug hello.

I clench my jaw and speak through it. "Why are you showing this to me?"

"I told you that you were no better than me. Except my assistant wasn't also a whore who slept her way around Atlanta. Do you know she begged me for a job at *Emulation* while she was riding my cock? Said she would do anything. Her tight little body felt good wrapped around me. She stopped by last week, in fact. Loves it when I call her filthy names and degrade her."

My heart sinks to my stomach. She knows I don't get along with my dad. She wouldn't do this to me—to us! My muscles are wound tight, and I can feel the blood trying to pump through my body. Everything feels upside down.

I shake my head, not believing him. "You're lying."

"What gain do I have by lying? I'm doing you a favor. I've heard rumors you're sleeping with her and wanted you to know the truth about what type of girl she really is before you get in over your head. She's willing to play any side she can to get ahead. Imagine what other board members she might be sleeping with to secure a nice paycheck?

"Anyway, I was able to dig this past information up easily. Imagine what someone else could do with it?"

I ball my hand into a fist and slam it down on top of the desk. "This was nine years ago, before I took over for you. Even if someone decided to look into this, it doesn't change anything." *No, but the fact that she's sleeping with you does.*

"No, not for you. But some of the people on those lists would prefer to keep their nighttime indiscretions hidden from the public eye."

"Again, it was nine years ago," I grit through my teeth, trying to rein my anger in.

"This information is, but isn't your little secretary still working at a strip club? I'm sure if she's sleeping with me, then she's still sleeping with men there. It's only a matter of time before your name is associated with her nightlife, and the board kicks you out, too. Or clients start dropping you like flies." He gives a heavy sigh. "I'm sorry you had to find out this way. I just found out when I gave you the information after I heard rumors that the two of you are an item."

My mind is reeling with all this new information. The picture of her sitting on my dad's lap stares me right in the face, and I scrunch my face in disgust.

For once in his life, what he's saying holds some weight. I need to fix this before it's too late and I end up dragging the company down. "What do I need to do?"

CHAPTER 31

ADDISON

By the time I get to *RISE*, I've calmed down only a fraction. I still can't believe Ethan would have the audacity to call me a whore. I mean, yes, according to the definition, I am, but he knows I'm not proud of my past. But there's not a chance in hell that man is going to tell me how to live my life.

What he doesn't understand is I make more owning this place than the salary he gives me. *Not that I'd ever tell him that.* I love my job at *Emulation*. It's challenging and keeps me engaged. I've been working at *RISE* for so long, I'm almost bored with it. The business side of it is always the same, but working with Ethan is different, more rewarding in a way.

I storm through the empty space and see Danny putting some glasses away behind the bar. He offers a wave in greeting, and I all but ignore him to get to the back room. I look at the schedule for dances tonight and see I'm on twice to cover for Quinlin, who called in sick.

I've thought about calling or texting Ethan only about a hundred times, but I know if *I'm* this pissed off, he probably is, too. I'm not a damn whore, and I know he knows that, but it still hurt to hear it from him. I'm not even sure if we are still on for tomorrow for the cookout. *God, I need a drink.*

Dancing tonight will be good. I can clear my head and figure out how I want to attack this problem. I take a deep, cleansing breath through my nose and hold it for a beat, then release it slowly. I do this a few more times, relaxing each one of my muscles as I do it until I finally feel like myself again.

I get into my outfit for the night—a sexy pink teddy, white thong, and white heels. I like to switch it up every now and again, and tonight just feels like an innocent sex-kitten kind of night. I pin my wig into place and place my mask over my eyes, securing it behind my head. I turn in front of the floor-length mirror, looking at myself before I head up to the back office to get some paperwork done.

There are a few invoices on the desk I've been meaning to pay, but haven't gotten around to yet. The business side of things should keep me busy until it's my turn to hit the stage.

I'VE BEEN SO ABSORBED IN WHAT I'M BEEN DOING, I DON'T HEAR the knock on the door, so I jump when Sarah starts talking to me. I place my hand over my frantic heartbeat and shake my head at her. "Jesus, you scared me."

"Sorry, just wanted you to know you're up next."

"Thanks, I'll be right there." I lock up the computer and file a few items away so the other girls know they've been taken care of. Although, it seems like it's just Eden and myself here more and more. Our small group is starting to divide.

Lia's let this place take a back seat to being a mother, and I couldn't be happier for her. She deserves it. I'm glad she's focused on her precious little girl. Everleigh has done the same, taking time to be with Luca and Rory. She's not going to want to keep doing this either. Things will never be how they were before, and the older I get, the more I'm okay with that. This place is our salvation, it always will be, but maybe it's time to turn the spotlight off for a while.

I sigh, thinking about the fight with Ethan. I don't want to be here doing any of this anymore either. Not when it makes him upset. I don't want him to think I'm cheating on him, or doing this because I'm not happy with him. Both are the complete opposite of how I feel. I'm stubborn, just like a jackass, my mom used to tell me.

I grab my phone and send a quick text message to Ethan.

Me: *I'm sorry.*

The music changes, letting me know my set is about to start. I hurry out onto the dark stage and focus all my energy into the song and the intricate moves. Tonight, I'm dancing for me. I wrap my leg around the pole and balance myself on one heel as I wait for the lights to come up. I take one more deep breath and begin spinning.

The music is some upbeat pop song, but I don't even hear the lyrics. I'm too caught up in the thrum of the bass and beat. I grab onto the pole and lift my legs out to either side, wrapping them around the warm metal. I drop my hands to lean back, scanning the crowd as I spin slowly around, showing off for the crowd.

A few men are already asking for private dances; I can tell the moment they call a girl to their table as I continue to gyrate my hips and make love to the audience. They are eating it up tonight. I'm at the end of my set when I catch his stare. The most beautiful brown eyes I've ever seen.

Ethan.

He came. My heart is so full it takes all my strength to not run off the stage and into his arms to apologize. I want to forget this day ever happened. I know he didn't mean what he said; it was in the heat of the moment. I keep my eyes locked on his as the song comes to an end and the lights dim.

Candy comes up to the side of the stage to tell me several gentlemen have requested private dances, but I tell her I'm not in the mood. I'm only here to cover a shift, nothing more, so I rush past her and into the audience, looking for him.

I find him stalking toward me, and I turn to lead him to my room. When we reach the door, he pushes me inside and slams it, hard. I smell tequila on his breath and push back on his chest as he presses his weight into me.

"You're drunk," I whisper. I'm not afraid of him. I know he would never hurt me, even when we're angry at one another.

He pulls my mask off and throws it on the floor, his nostrils flaring with anger as his warm breath fans across my face. I reach forward to touch his cheek, but he wraps his large hand around my wrist and pins it to the wall above my head, doing the same with the other, holding them in one hand.

His fingers trace down my flat stomach, and he pushes my panties to the side, shoving his fingers in aggressively. It doesn't matter, though, because, from the moment I saw him tonight, I was wet. I grunt at the intrusion, but he gives me a dark smile.

"So wet already, Addy?" I can't do anything but nod, my brain too slow to catch up.

He finger-fucks me hard and fast, barely giving me a moment to breathe. He bites on my neck and sucks the skin between my neck and collarbone. No doubt he's leaving his mark, and it turns me on even more. I struggle in his grasp as his thumb starts circling my clit.

"Come on, Addy. Where's my dirty girl? Come for me, baby."

I shudder at his words. They are so dark, so unlike him, yet I can't help the way my body is attuned to him, and I come hard, soaking his hand. He removes his fingers and traces my lips, making me taste my salty essence. He undoes his pants and spins me around, pulls my thong to the side, and sinks into me.

I moan and he shoves his fingers into my mouth. I suck and lap at them, knowing how much he loves the dirty side of me. *This make-up sex is so damn hot.* His hand slides down my throat and he squeezes. I tense under his touch. He's never been this aggressive before, this dirty.

"Relax, baby," he coos as he thrusts hard and fast. "Do you hear my cock sliding in and out of your wet pussy, baby? You're so fucking hot like this, under my control."

God damn, when did this man get so good at dirty talk?

"Make me come, Ethan," I moan.

He pulls out suddenly, and I gasp in shock. I try to turn around, but he holds me against the wall, spits on his hand, and rubs it around my puckered hole. *Jesus, he's going to kill me tonight.* I press my ass out more as he lines himself up with my back entrance and presses in.

I tense up. "Oh fuck, Ethan. Slow down." I press my hand back on top of his thigh to slow him and give me a second to catch my breath, but he starts thrusting and squeezes my throat again, cutting off enough air supply it sends my over-worked and on-edge body into another orgasm. Every muscle in my body tenses, and I have a hard time staying on my feet. No sex has *ever* felt like this. I feel as if I'm floating on a cloud, the sensations too much. He bites down on my shoulder as he comes deep inside me and stills.

I press my forehead to the wall, catching my breath. That was some of the most intense make-up sex I have ever experienced. I turn to him with a smile on my face, expecting to see the same sated look on his, but his scowl is back in place. He pulls a wad of cash out of his wallet and tosses it on the chair next to me.

My chin trembles as I reach out for him. He pulls back, a look of pure disgust blanketing his features. "You really are nothing more than a whore, Addison. I can't believe I fell for you and your deceiving tricks."

"What?" I ask, my voice cracking as tears stream down my face. "Ethan, I told you—"

"That you've been sleeping with my dad behind my back? No, you forgot to mention that little tidbit." He takes a step closer, and I take a small one back, keeping a small amount of distance between us. "Is that how you moved up in the company? Are you the way my father has been keeping his claws in me and the company?" His nostrils flare again. His anger is palatable and hangs in the air between us. The energy rolling off him in waves makes me shiver.

"No, I-I didn't," I wipe my eyes. "I'm not." I can't even think straight. All the words coming out of his mouth aren't registering, aren't making any sense to me. My throat feels thick, and I can't swallow. "Who told you?"

"Who *told* me? Are you fucking kidding me?" he bellows.

A loud knock on the door startles us before a large man comes rushing in. He grabs Ethan and starts to drag him outside. I sink to my knees on the ground, tears running down my face. The one man I've loved for most of my adult life hates me for something I didn't even do.

CHAPTER 32

ETHAN

I'm thrown out on my ass with a message that my membership has been suspended and not to return. *Not like I need this drama in my life anyway.* Sleeping with a stripper is what got me into this mess in the first place. I'm too drunk to drive home, but at least it's done. My brain and my heart war with one another, and I can't keep up with the emotions swirling around inside of me. Although some of that might be the half a bottle of tequila I tossed back.

Dad told me he would stop sleeping with Addison and would bury the other information from the board; I just had to break up with her. Simple enough, right? The *only* girl who I've felt anything for in my life, so let's rip her away from me, too. Perfect ending for this fucked up night.

I remember mentioning my dad to her once, and she tensed up, didn't even want to tell me about it. And now I know why. She was fucking him and didn't want me to know about it. How can she be okay with doing that to me... to us?

I stare at my phone, the bright screen making it hard to read anything. I need to get my ass out of here. I can't call

Landry because Lia and Addy are friends. No way I want to be anywhere close to people she knows. I could try Cal, but I think he told me something about doing a photoshoot in Colombia or some shit like that. Who knows?

When you're a workaholic, there aren't many hours left in the day for friends, and after those two, I'm tapped out. I have a few other people I talk to, but none of them are local. *God, this is so lame.* I open my contacts and hover over my mom's name. She always used to tell me, if I run into any problems, call her.

I hope that's still true.

She answers after a few rings, her voice thick with sleep. "Ethan, are you okay, honey?"

"No, I'm really not. Can you come get me? I'm too drunk to drive, and I can't stand to see any of my friends right now."

"Where are you?"

I don't want to tell her I'm at a strip club, so I walk a few blocks down the street to a gas station and wait for her there. While I wait, I stare at the last message from Addison. I saw it right as I got to the club. It's like she knew I would find out about the skeletons in her closet and call her out for it.

Is she even actually sorry for what she did, what she *continues* to do? My anger starts to rise again, like a lead weight in my chest. I rub the spot over my heart and start to calm down when I see Mom's sedan pulling into a spot.

I slide into the passenger side and close the door without saying a word. After a few minutes of her driving, I finally speak. "Can I stay at your place tonight? I don't want to go home."

She nods and glances over at me, concern etched on her face. "Of course. Anything you want to talk about? Girl problems?"

I huff and rub my forehead, trying to keep my headache at

bay. "Yeah, something like that. I don't want to talk about it right now."

She nods again and stays silent, so the only noise is the passing of cars and the soft rock station Mom is listening to. I close my eyes and lean my head back against the headrest. I think about the night, replaying the events in my head.

Is it possible she was telling the truth? God, she seemed so upset tonight. I wanted to pull her into my arms, kiss the top of her head, and tell her it's going to be okay. I wanted to tell her we'd get through this together—figure it out. Thanks to Mr. Tequila sitting in my stomach, though, he did the talking. *Fucker.*

No way of knowing now. I spoke with Aiden in human resources before I left for the day and told him she's not working out as my assistant and needs to be transferred on Monday. I need to keep my distance from her, for the good of the company and the good of my sanity.

Mom pulls into the garage, and I get out, dragging my heavy feet into the house. She fills a glass of water, hands it to me, and kisses me on the cheek.

"Drink that and get some rest. Things will look brighter in the morning. And then we'll talk about why you were at a strip club when you brought home that nice girl Addison not too long ago." She places her hand on my forearm and pulls the side of my head down to her lips for a kiss, then heads upstairs without another word.

I drink the glass of water, then have a second one for good measure before trekking up the stairs to my old bedroom. There is still a bed here, but it's no longer my room. She's converted it into a guest bedroom, so all my sports posters and random baseball trophies are in the attic. I take off my shirt and pants to lay down in just my boxers.

I shift a few times, trying to find a comfortable position to lay in, but I don't expect sleep to come easily for me. I grab my phone and text Dad.

Me: *It's done.*

Those two words make it seem so final. Addison deserves so much better than Paul Freeman. There's no doubt in my mind that her sleeping with him wasn't her idea, and that he might be holding this same information over her head as well.

I should have let her explain. That's the last thought that trickles through my mind before the world grows heavy and I fall into a restless sleep.

I WAKE THE NEXT MORNING TO THE SMELL OF COFFEE, BACON, and pancakes. *Mom's comfort food always makes me feel better.* I drag myself out of bed and put on my clothes from last night since I have nothing else to change into. I glance at my phone and see I have a message from Dad, but I can't bring myself to look at it right now. I'm too disgusted.

I climb down the stairs, my headache not as terrible as I thought it would be, thanks to the water before falling into bed last night. I step into the kitchen, and my mom looks at me, a warm smile on her face. "How'd you sleep?"

"Like shit. Breakfast smells good." I sit at one of the high-top chairs at the breakfast nook, and Mom places another glass of water and two aspirin in front of me. I take the pills and finish the glass of water.

"So, are we going to talk about what happened now or later?"

How about never? I know that answer won't fly with her, and she'll drag it out of me sooner rather than later. Probably best to rip the Band-aid off and get it over with.

So, I do my best to recount the details of yesterday. Mom

listens as we eat breakfast, only asking the occasional question here and there, just to make sure she stays on top of the story. I omit the part about Dad having sex with my girlfriend, but I do tell her about Addison being an owner of *RISE*.

"Ethan, I'm sure there's information you're keeping from me. I don't need to know the intimate details of your life, but everything you're telling me does *not* sound like the girl I met. The girl *I* met was charming, kind, and loves you. The moment you two walked through the door, I could see it. I said to myself, *that's* the girl for my boy." She places her hand on my arm and gives it a few pats before reaching for her coffee.

I run my fingers through my messy hair, rumpling it more. "Honestly, Mom, I thought so, too. She lost her whole family in a fire over ten years ago, and she took me home to Virginia to share that part of her life with me." I offer a sad smile as I think about the trip a week ago. Everything was so right, and I felt like we were moving in the same direction, both of us wanting the same things.

But now…

"Did you ask her to explain her side of things last night?"

I hang my head in shame. "No. I couldn't see past my drunken stupor."

"Talk to her, Ethan. There's nothing you can do that's so bad that it can't be fixed." She smiles warmly. "You may have to do some begging, but it can be fixed."

"I don't know, Mom. I said some really shitty things and hurt her pretty bad last night." *Like calling her a whore.*

"We all say and do things we don't mean. It's how we handle the fallout and aftermath that defines us."

CHAPTER 33

ADDISON

I'm not even sure how I got home last night. Brian, my assigned security guard, came barreling into my room last night after Ethan took me roughly and tossed money at me like I was worthless. I laid on the floor crying for what felt like hours. I vaguely remember Eden coming into my room and laying down on the floor behind me, holding me. Someone must have called her because she wasn't on the schedule last night.

She asked me several times if I wanted to talk about it, and when I refused, she helped me over to the bed and tucked me under the covers, telling me she'd be back. I know she asked about what happened so she could help. She's always protected us girls, been like a mother hen to us.

She came back into the room a while later with my stuff, and I felt a strong pair of arms lift me up, cradling me against a firm chest. I didn't have to open my eyes to know it wasn't Ethan coming back to say he was sorry and let me explain.

No.

Ethan was gone.

My past messed everything up, just like I feared it would.

God, why the hell didn't I tell him all my secrets sooner? This all could have been avoided because then he would know I was telling the truth and that there was no one else—hasn't been since we got together. I would never do that to him.

I love him.

That thought makes the tears fall down my cheeks, landing on the soft pillow below my head. Sobs wrack my body, and I shiver under the blankets, wrapping my arms around myself. My phone dings from the nightstand, but I don't have the energy to look at it, nor do I care. I want to wallow in this self-pity for as long as I can.

What the hell am I going to do on Monday? I can't keep working for him, not when he thinks I'm sleeping with clients and, even worse, *his dad*. God, I would never touch that man again. The lap dance he got was enough, but when he tried to force me to have sex with him, I was done.

I can only imagine the lies Paul told Ethan about me to have him react the way he did. What did I ever do to him to make him hate me so much? I would love to drive to his house and ask him why he wants to ruin his son's life, but I don't want to see his face.

My phone buzzes again just as there's a knock on my front door. "Go away," I call out from my room. I know I'm too far away for the person to hear me, but it doesn't stop me from doing it and pulling the covers over my head.

I hear my front door unlock, and there is only one person it can be—Eden. All the girls still have a key to my place, but Eden and Everleigh are the only ones who would actually use it. Since Everleigh is probably still cuddled up in bed with Luca, that leaves Eden.

She pulls the covers down from my head, and when I try to pull them back up, she rips the whole comforter off the bed.

"Get up."

"Fuck you, Eady. Leave me alone." I turn away from her and curl up again. She smacks my ass hard, and I barely flinch.

"Harder, Roxie. You know I like a bit of pain," I mock her.

"Don't make me pull out my whip. You're not gonna stay here and wallow in self-pity. Ethan was an asshole last night, and he's lucky I wasn't there to shove my boot up his ass, but there's nothin' you can do about it right now. You both need time to cool down and then discuss everything."

I turn and glare before getting up to stand in front of her. She has only about an inch or two on me, but even she seems to shrink back with the anger rolling off me. I keep my voice low and even. "He fucked my ass, called me a whore, and threw money at me. Not sure there's much to discuss there. So, I suggest you march your ass out of this Goddamned apartment right now before I do something I regret." I point to the door.

Her brows crease as my words sink in, and pity takes over her features. "I'm sorry, Addy."

"Nothing to be sorry for. It's my fault for not opening up to him sooner and telling him everything about my past. I honestly didn't think it would be that big of a deal, especially when I had the chance to explain, but he never gave that to me. I've been in love with a man who I didn't even really know." I shrug and walk to the bathroom. "Please don't be here when I get out."

I close the door behind me and lock it.

I TAKE A LONGER SHOWER THAN NEEDED, ONLY GETTING OUT because I run out of hot water. I contemplate hanging out in the cold water, but my body repels the idea, and I start to shake under the spray. I wrap a fluffy towel around me and look at my reflection in the mirror. I still look like the same girl from last night, but I feel as if I've aged a hundred years.

My phone is buzzing like crazy on my nightstand, and I finally drag myself away from the mirror to look at it.

Missed calls from Eden, Everleigh, Lia, and Aiden from work.

Why the hell is Aiden calling me on a Saturday? I ignore my best friends for now, knowing they are all calling to threaten to kick Ethan's ass all the way to kingdom come. I don't need to listen to that right now in an attempt to make me feel better.

I call Aiden, and he picks up almost instantly. "Girl, the fuck did you do?" he asks.

I shake my head. *Apparently, a lot that I'm unaware of.* "I have no idea, why? What's going on?"

"I got an email from Ethan yesterday, requesting your transfer to a different department. What the hell happened? The rumor is you guys have been sleeping together, but I didn't want to ask you if it's true. I figured you would tell me."

He's transferring me. This day is already shaping up to be wonderful.

"We are. Actually, we were dating, but things went south last night. You know what, though, Aiden? I'm quitting anyway. I'll draft up a letter and drop it off on his desk today when I go to clear out my stuff."

Aiden lowers his voice. "What are you going to do?"

I lay down on my bed, my wet hair sprawled against the pillow. My chin quivers, and I wipe at my eyes, then take a deep breath and clear my throat. "I already have another job lined up."

"Addy…" he trails off.

"It's fine, Aiden. Thanks for the heads up. I'll make sure to leave my letter with Mr. Freeman, and I'll also email you a copy for my HR record. I gotta go. We'll chat later, maybe get together for some drinks. Bye."

I hang up before he can get another word in.

I thought Ethan was my savior, my white knight. Turns out he's just a loser in tinfoil like the rest of them.

I press the palms of my hands over my eyes, stopping the sting of tears. *He's not worth it.* Maybe if I say those words enough, I'll start to believe them.

CHAPTER 34

ETHAN

After talking with my mom, my head is a little clearer. I hung around with her for a few hours but decided to head home early in the afternoon. I try to call Addison, but after one ring, it goes to voicemail.

"Addison, I'm so sorry about last night. Everything about it was fucked up, and I acted like a complete asshole. I'm not asking for forgiveness, because I know I haven't earned that. I just want a chance to explain. Call me."

I hang up, hoping she calls me back and I can see her before Landry and Lia's cookout. I will grovel at her feet if I have to. Addison Snyder is the best damn thing that has ever happened to me, and I was a fucking fool for treating her like I did. In my tequila daze last night, I couldn't see it.

I pace back and forth in my house, unable to stop the nervous energy coursing through my veins. Nothing short of being able to see her and hold her again is going to make me be able to relax.

I try texting her, but I'm not surprised when a half-hour later I still haven't received a message back. I hop in my car and drive to Landry's, hoping I can get her alone to talk with her privately. I pull into the driveway and try Addison one more time—nothing. Her car isn't in the driveway, but she could have gotten a ride from one of her friends. On a resounding sigh, I get out and knock on the door.

Landry answers, and his easygoing smile fades as he sees me. *Guess good news travels fast.* "H-hey, Ethan. I didn't think you were coming after—"

"Is she here? I really need to talk with her." I look past him into the house and when he doesn't answer right away, push past him. I make it about two steps inside when Eden steps in front of me, her arms crossed over her chest.

"You've got a lot of balls showing up here today, Ethan, after treating my best friend like a prostitute and throwing money at her."

I rub my forehead. "I need to talk with her."

She steps closer, and I take a small one back, trying to keep space between us. "You don't get that right anymore. Not after how you treated her." She shakes her head in disgust. "Addison has a heart of gold, and she trusted you with it, but you trampled over it instead."

"I know—"

She holds her hand up in front of my face and points her finger at me. "You ruined her. She's been in love with you for nine years." She holds nine fingers up, emphasizing her point. "I never want to see your face around here, or anywhere close to her, again."

I push her finger out of my face and shake my head, keeping my features stoic. "You're not her protector. She's a big girl."

"You're right. She's a big girl and can fight her own battles, but that doesn't mean she doesn't deserve an army standing behind her."

Lia and Everleigh step into view, their arms crossed over their chests in defiance, and I turn to see Landry. He holds his hands up as if to say 'don't get me involved'.

"Hey, man, maybe it's best if you go," Landry says.

I nod. I know it's best to lay low for a while. If these girls are *anything* like Addison, they will fight like hell to protect one another. Any other time, I'd admire that trait, but right now, it's keeping me from Addison and just pisses me off.

Landry holds the door open for me, and when I walk through, he steps out behind me and closes the door.

"Is she in there, Lan? Will you at least tell me so I know she's safe? She won't answer any of my calls or texts… not that I blame her. I wouldn't talk to me either after how I treated her."

He shakes his head with a somber look. "She's not here. She texted Lia a little while ago and said something has come up and she can't make it." I nod and turn to get into my car. "I know these girls, Ethan. I don't know all their stories, but I can tell you what I do know. These ladies see one another as sisters. If one is hurting, all of them are hurting. Whatever you did with Addison—"

"You don't know? I'm shocked news hasn't spread yet."

He smirks and nods. "Yeah, I know. I was trying to be a pal and not bring it up. What you did hurt not only Addison; you hurt all of them. *RISE* is something they built from the ground up, and they are damn proud of it. What you see, the show they put on, it's fake. Don't judge a book by its appearance, you know?"

I nod, understanding what he's trying to say, but keep my eyes to the ground. I rub the back of my neck, trying to ease some of the tension. "Yeah, I know."

"Give her time. Give them time."

"Would you do me a favor?" I look up at him, hoping he'll at least give me this. He nods once.

"Would you at least make sure she's safe for me? I won't ask you where she is, just that she's okay and not physically hurt or anything."

"When I hear anything, I'll let you know." He clasps his hand on my shoulder and gives me a gentle squeeze before letting go. "Be prepared to be castrated before you get her back, man."

Duly noted.

I'm almost home when I get an email notification from Aiden in HR. The subject line reads: Addison Snyder's Notice of Resignation.

"Fuck!" I yell as I slam my hand down on the steering wheel. I press my foot on the gas pedal to get to the office as quickly as I can. I'm sure, if she gave her notice, she's at the office packing up her desk. I can cut her off and tell her I don't accept.

I dial her number, and like before, it rings once before going to voicemail. "I don't accept your notice to leave. We need to talk about this. Call me. I'm on my way into the office." I toss my phone into the passenger seat in frustration.

How did I mess things up so badly? It's because I listened to my fucking father. I never should have done that. Those pictures had to have been fabricated. There's no way she would do that. She wouldn't have opened up to me about her past and her family if she was planning on ruining anything that was happening between us.

Nothing makes sense right now. I've always been able to solve puzzles, but Addison Snyder is the one I can't figure out. Not without seeing and talking to her. I cut a car off trying to get to the exit, and he honks at me before flipping me off. *Fuck you, too, buddy.*

I pull into the garage and see that her car is there. My heart is beating so fast in my chest it feels like I've run a marathon. I run to the elevator and hit the button several times, willing the damn thing to get here faster. I would opt for the stairs, but by the time I could make it to the top, I'm sure she'll be gone.

The office space is quiet and mostly dark, except for the light in my office. My heart squeezes in my chest. *I haven't missed her.*

"Addy," I call out for her, with no response. I jog down the hall and slow when I see her bare desk. All her pictures and small trinkets have been removed. All that is left is her phone, computer, and a lamp. I walk into my office, praying to God I'll find her sitting there, but all I find instead is a letter addressed to me in a sealed envelope. I rip open the seal and unfold the paper to read it.

Mr. Freeman,

I am writing to announce my resignation from Emulation, effective immediately.

This was not an easy decision to make. The past five years at this company have been very rewarding, and I have learned so much working here. I've enjoyed working for you and managing a very hectic schedule to make sure your job was easier.

Thank you for the opportunities for growth you have provided. I wish you and the company all the best.

Sincerely,

Addison Snyder

There is another sheet of paper behind it, written in her pretty handwriting.

Ethan,

I'm not sure exactly what happened yesterday, except that you learned more about my past than I had been willing to share. I was going to tell you everything after this weekend, but I was scared of what you would think. Some of what you heard is true, I imagine, but I never slept with your father. I'm NOT sleeping with your father. I have not thought about or slept with another man since you came into my life and we started seeing one another. I would never do anything like that to hurt you.

I'm sorry for everything, but I'm especially sorry I didn't tell you about my past with your father sooner. I did what I had to do to get by, and at times, I'm not proud of it. I have been in love with you since the first time I met you almost ten years ago. You were my reason for pressing on and seeing light at the end of the tunnel. Most men treated me like nothing but a stripper, but you saw a glimpse of the girl underneath. The real me.

I hurt you, and for that, I can never forgive myself. I didn't mean to, and I hope one day you can forgive me. Aiden told me I was being transferred, but if I can't work with you, I don't want to work at Emulation. Take care, I wish you all the best. You'll always hold a piece of my heart.

XoXo

Your Addy

I drop down into my seat and read her words over and over. My body breaks out in a cold sweat, and my blood runs cold. She can't do this to me. I *won't* let her do this to me.

I pick up my phone and dial the one person responsible for this whole thing—my dad.

"Why the fuck did you lie to me?" I seethe.

"About what exactly?"

"Addison and you sleeping together." My teeth are clenched so hard I'm surprised I can get the words out.

"That girl's past is going to ruin your reputation, and the

board will kick you out. I've done you a favor by making you see the person she really is."

"You *lied* about her. The only thing that proves is I'm right not to trust you."

"I lied about her and me, not about the rest of that list. She's a PR nightmare waiting to happen. I'm just looking out for you. I built this company from the ground up, and I'm not about to let a board of assholes ruin my legacy by kicking you out, too."

"Do me a favor. Stay the fuck out of my life and never talk to me again."

CHAPTER 35

ADDISON

Ethan's car is parked right next to mine in the garage by the time I get there with my small box of stuff. I look around me for him, and when I don't see him, I take a deep breath. Tears start to fall from my eyes again as I put my stuff in the back seat and get in.

I promised I would stop by Lia's for something to eat, not that I really want to, but I know the girls are worried about me. I'll be fine, though. I make enough money at *RISE* that I don't need to worry about being homeless anytime soon, and if I want to look for another job, I have time to do it.

I pull out of the garage as quickly as possible to get over to Lia's. I want to get this over with so I can eat my weight in ice cream, and maybe follow it with a bottle of wine. Sounds like the perfect evening to me.

I wish my mom was here. She would know what to do. Tears well in my eyes again as I get off the highway and change directions.

I want to go home.

I pick up my phone and call Eden.

"Hey, you doing okay?" she asks, her voice full of concern.

"I'm going home for a few days."

"Like, your apartment?" she asks, confused.

"No. Virginia. I need to be alone for a bit and get my head on straight again. I need time away from everyone and everything to do it. I'll be careful, but I wanted you to know where I was going so you don't barge into my apartment and freak out when I'm not there."

"Addy, you don't have to do this. Want me to come with you?"

"No, but I need this. I'll text you when I get there so you know I'm safe. Love you."

She sighs but knows she's not going to change my mind. "Love you, too. Be safe and text me. You know I worry."

"Promise."

I merge onto I-84 north and turn up the music to drown out the sound of my breaking heart. I blocked his number first thing this morning, and if I know Ethan, he's probably been trying to get in touch with me. Especially if he gets the note I left him. I don't have anything more to say to him right now.

I need time alone.

I need time to heal.

⸻

IT'S A LONG DRIVE TO VIRGINIA, BUT I'VE MANAGED TO MAKE IT up here in record time. *Thank God there were no cops out to stop me from going far over the speed limit.* I need to stop at a store and get some clothes and toiletries before I look for a place to stay for a few nights.

I sit in a Target parking lot and pull up my blocked list, hovering over Ethan's name. I wonder how many messages he left before he realized I'd blocked him? If I was a stronger woman, I would move on and forget, but I'm not. My entire being is drawn to him like a moth to a flame.

I open up the voicemails and scroll to the bottom to see I have ten blocked number voicemails. I put my hand over my mouth and stifle a sob. *They are all from Ethan.* I don't even have to listen to know they are all from him.

This is the worst form of torture, but I can't help myself. Like watching a train wreck happening, I click on the button to listen.

"Addison, I'm so sorry about last night. Everything about it was fucked up, and I acted like a complete asshole. I'm not asking for forgiveness, because I know I haven't earned that. I just want a chance to explain. Call me."

I delete the message and the next one starts to play.

"I don't accept your notice to leave. We need to talk about this. Call me. I'm on my way into the office." I hear the anger in his voice as he tries to control his temper.

I delete that one, too. Over and over—listen and delete. The voicemails get more frantic each time, and each time he sounds more defeated. It's breaking my heart knowing I'm causing him all this pain. I close my eyes and lean my head back against the headrest as I click play on the final message.

"Addy. I'm so sorry. I can't say it enough for you to ever forgive me. I don't deserve it. I was angry, and hurt, and a fucking bastard. You deserve to be with a man who will love and cherish you for everything you are and not judge you on your past. I always thought I was that man, but it turns out I couldn't be what you needed.

"I want you to know I found out the truth from my dad. He gave me a list with all these men's names on it, and I went ballistic when he said they were old clients. I knew you slept with men—hell, you slept with me at the club, but when I saw the list, it made it so real. I know you need time to sort through your feelings and where we

stand. Just know, if you come back to me, I promise I will work a life-time to prove to you I'm the man you need.

He takes a deep breath and sniffles into the phone. *"Mom told me the moment she saw you, she knew you were special and the one. I love the idea of you being the one for me, getting to wake up to your beautiful face every day, making love to you every night. That sounds like a dream come true.*

"I'll wait for you, Addy. However long you need. You're my forever... if you'll have me. I love you, and I was a fool for not telling you before now. If you give me another chance, you can bet I'll rectify that."

The tears fall so hard and fast down my face as the message ends. My heart has been shattered into a million pieces, and I'm not sure I'll ever be able to put them back where they go. I just want to sleep until the pain dissipates.

I take a few minutes to get my crying under control, put on my big girl panties, and step out of the car. Crying never solved anything. Only time and experience, and maybe a good pair of stripper heels.

CHAPTER 36

ETHAN

I've been sitting at Addison's empty desk with her letter in my hand for the better part of two hours. I've left her ten voicemails and texted her numerous times without any response. I'm not an idiot; I know she blocked my number, not that I blame her. I would have done the same thing.

Landry: *Heard Addy went home to Virginia.*

Me: *Thanks for the heads up.*

Landry: *The girls are worried about her.*

Me too, Landry.

Me: *I'm going to fix this. I promise.*

Virginia. I'm not surprised she went home. I hate the fact that she's running. I hate that *I'm* the reason she's running. I pull up flights. The next one doesn't leave until six tomorrow morning. It's about a seven-hour ride, and there's no way I'll be able to make that drive tonight and still be coherent to see her tomorrow morning. The flight is my best option.

Hopefully, it will also give her some time to cool down so we can talk this out. *And I can beg her to forgive my stupid ass.* I can't believe I took my dad's word over hers. I'm such a fucking idiot. I haven't trusted that man in over five years, so why did now seem like a good time?

He didn't lie about everything...

No. He didn't lie about some of her clients, but I don't give a shit about them. I know enough about her time at *The Devil's Playground* to understand the type of situation she was thrust into. Well, some of her situation, anyway.

My phone rings, and it's Clive Demurs, one of the board members.

"Hi, Clive, what can I do for you?"

"Ethan, we've received some news today about a girl whom you've been seeing, and I wanted to talk to you about it."

I give a resounding sigh. "We broke up, and she gave her notice. No need to drag me down memory lane, Clive."

"Are you aware she was one of Vince Perelli's girls at the strip club and has slept with a lot of big, potential clients? Clients we have been trying to get for some time?"

Where the fuck is he going with this? "I'm aware she was a stripper. She hasn't done that in a long time, but I'm aware of her past."

Vince Perelli was killed almost ten years ago and was part of a lot of dirty business here in Atlanta. The rumor was he was big in the mafia and involved in things such as money laundering, sex trafficking, and murder.

Sex trafficking. Was Addy trafficked? Did I fuck a girl who had no other choice? My mind starts racing as I try to think back to when I met her. She was one of the highlights of the show.

Vince was the owner of *The Devil's Playground*. I remember Dad talking about him like they were such great friends, how he was such a stand-up guy. There were four girls that he called his little birdies.

Jesus.

Fucking.

Christ.

Addison, Eden, Everleigh, and Magnolia were the girls—his little birdies. He used those girls to get ahead. I was so young at the time; I couldn't even see what was right in front of me. She seemed so willing and eager. *Of course, she was eager. She was probably trained to be like that.* I stand from the desk suddenly, and my head spins.

Clive hums through the receiver, and I completely forgot he was still there. I want to reach through the phone and strangle him. "Get her back working for *Emulation*."

I'm stunned by his response. I'm not even sure how to respond to him. He wants me to get her back here so we can what, exploit sex from her to gain clients? Up until this exact moment, I never realized how horrible and corrupt this company truly was. I knew there were clients we entertained who weren't exactly on the straight and narrow, but this crosses so many lines.

"No."

He sighs. "There's a board meeting on Monday, and if you don't have her back with the company, willing to help procure some of these high-profile clients, I can't secure your spot as CEO. Think about it. I'm sure you'll make the right choice."

The phone disconnects, and I stand there, staring at the wall. The only way I can save my ass at this company is if I pimp out my ex-girlfriend and become no better than the people who shaped her past. Up until this moment, I never fully understood the type of situation she was thrust into, but now I do. I'll be damned if I put her back there.

PULLING INTO THE GRAVEYARD, I FOLLOW THE SAME PATH WE took only a week ago. *Was it really only a week ago we were here?* It seems like forever ago, and at the same time, like no time has passed at all. I slow the car and park a short distance away from the spot where Addison cried her eyes out, but I refuse to get out.

She's here. I watch her from a distance. She's so beautiful sitting on the grass in front of the headstones that I pull my phone out to snap a picture of her. Her dark hair is piled high in a messy bun on top of her head, and she has on a pair of yoga pants and a fitted t-shirt. As she sits cross-legged, I watch her lips move, talking to her family.

My body is drawn to her, and I want to get out to wrap her in my arms, but she needs this time. I'm afraid if I try to push her, she will push back, and then I will lose her for good.

I can't.

I won't lose her.

So, I wait patiently in my car until she finally stands, pulls a few weeds out of the ground around the light stones, and turns her back to me to get into her car. When she drives off, I get out and take over the spot she was just occupying.

Addison had brought some fresh flowers with her and laid them down at the gravesite. I didn't want to show up empty-handed, so I made sure to get a few premade ones from Mrs. Robinson at the flower shop. She beamed when I walked into the store this morning.

I place the flowers down in front of the graves and read the dates again. Her parents were only in their late forties when they perished, and her brother was only fifteen. It's not fair that they were taken from her so early. I stand there and stare for a few minutes before I finally decide I should say something.

"Hi, Mr. and Mrs. Snyder, and Oliver. I'm sure Addison has told you everything that happened between us and how I royally fu—messed up things between us. I'm the biggest idiot in the world, and I don't deserve her." I sigh and look up at the sky. "I know I don't," I murmur as I shake my head.

"I know she needs time to heal, but I want you to know I'm going to do right by her. Addison has become an amazing, strong woman. You would be so proud of her and everything she has accomplished. She's a hard worker, and damn is she smart as a whip. She busted her ass to get her degree and always pushes the envelope.

"I'm going to win her back, and then I'm going to ask her to marry me. It might take me another ten years, but I'm willing to wait for her. She's it for me. I want you to know that. She is my happily ever after. Then, when I win her back, I'm going to be here with a ring to show you."

CHAPTER 37

ADDISON

After spending some much-needed time reflecting on everything, I feel ready to head back to Atlanta to face my decisions. I'm lucky to have *RISE* for now, but I know that's not going to be enough for me for long. I have too many ambitions and dreams to be stuck at the club for the rest of my life.

It's an overcast day; rain is supposed to be moving in soon. I want to hit the road so I can avoid it if possible. I drive to the graveyard to say my goodbyes before I head out of town again. I slow down and narrow my eyes as I get close to the plot. I see the flowers I put there, but there is another set at each of their headstones. I turn off the car and get out, walking up to the site I know so well.

There is a small sheet of paper under the flowers in front of my mom's grave, and I pick it up with shaky fingers.

You're the one, Addison. I'll do anything to prove it to you. I'll wait for you.

I look around for the familiar brown eyes that these words belong to. Ethan is here. He followed me. I know there is no way in hell the girls would have told him I came here, which means I only have Landry to blame.

Fresh tears fall from my eyes as I clutch the paper to my chest. My Ethan.

"Mom, what am I going to do?" I ask, looking to the sky. I wipe my face, and for a fleeting moment, the clouds part and the sun's rays shine down on me, the light seemingly focused on the small bit of paper in my hands. The parting closes, and I'm thrust into the cloudy morning again.

"I don't know if I can trust him again, Mom. The way he acted..."

I shake my head at my foolishness. I want to forgive him, call him, run to him so bad my heart aches. What am I going to do now?

Light raindrops fall on my cheeks and exposed arms. *Looks like the rain is coming a little sooner than I thought.* I slide my hand over the top of the three gravestones as a final parting and then climb back into my car. I pull up a new group chat with the girls to let them know I'm on my way back. Of course, Eden is the first to respond.

Eden: *You sure you don't need more time? We have everything taken care of here.*

Me: *No, I'm fine. I need to get back and get everything sorted out with my life. I'll see you in a while.*

EVEN THOUGH THE DRIVE WAS ABOUT SEVEN HOURS, I DON'T remember half of it. My mind was on a certain sexy CEO the entire time. At moments, my mind went to those dark places to relive the way he treated me when he thought I'd hurt him, but most of them were trying to sort him out. I pull into my parking spot at my apartment, and the doorman ushers me inside with a tip of his hat. I offer a small smile but continue on my way.

I stop at Eden's door, my hand poised and ready to knock to let her know I'm back, but decide against it at the last second. I need some time to sort everything out. I head for my apartment instead and plop down on the couch.

My phone rings with an unknown number, and I think about ignoring it, but pick it up at the last second instead.

"Hello?" I ask.

"Hello. Is this Ms. Snyder?" a male voice asks.

"Yes, who is this?"

"My name is Clive Dumurs."

Why is one of the board members from Emulation calling me? "I'm sorry, Mr. Dumurs, I am no longer with the company. I gave Mr. Freeman my notice, effective immediately."

"Yes, I heard. I have a proposition for you and wanted to know if you could come down to discuss it? I'll make it worth your time." Chills run down my spine with his words. *I'll make it worth your time.* Instantly, I feel cold and rub my arms to ward off the feeling. When I don't respond right away, he continues. "We have a job opening you would be perfect for. It would come with substantial compensation."

"Why isn't Aiden in HR contacting me about this opportunity?"

Warning. Warning.

"I wanted to speak with you personally about it."

"Does the position report directly to Mr. Freeman?"

"No, it doesn't. You would be working for me. How about you come down to the office tonight, after the workday, so we can discuss it in further detail? Please, Ms. Snyder. I'm just asking you to hear me out."

I sigh and relent, agreeing to come to the office at around six tonight to speak with him. I already know, whatever it is, I'm going to turn him down. I can't work at that company anymore. Especially if it would be working for Mr. Dumurs because I don't know if I could keep my heart from breaking if I saw Ethan every day.

I stroll up to the familiar building around five-fifty and take the elevator to the top floor, to the conference rooms. I notice a round, albeit tall man standing by the window, peering out over the Atlanta skyline. I rub my sweaty palms on my black dress slacks and tuck some hair behind my ear before pushing open the door like I own the place.

Rule one of being in business: self-confidence. I have no lack of that, especially when I channel my inner Madam Ember for this meeting. I did some research on him before I came here tonight—always know who you're dealing with.

He turns to face me, a fake smile plastered on his face. I straighten my spine as I stare him down, offering my own false smile in return. "Good evening, Mr. Dumurs."

"Thank you for coming, Ms. Snyder. Please, have a seat." He motions to the seat next to him, and I take it, pushing it a little further away to keep some distance between us.

"I'm sure you're aware this company is doing very well, and there are many prospective clients who want to work with us." I offer a small nod. "There are a lot of clients we have been trying to procure as well, clients who would make a world of a difference to have in our court. We've been trying to expand out into other cities across the United States."

He pulls out a binder with the list of business names and figures on them. I don't have to be a genius to realize the numbers are potential profits, and these aren't small numbers by any means.

I look up at him. "These are some hefty numbers and some big-name clients. What do you need me for? I'm just an executive assistant."

"It's recently come to light that you have certain... talents."

I quirk my eyebrow at that remark. "Talents?" His hand comes down over my wrist, and he squeezes when I try to pull out of his grasp. "Let. Go. Of. Me," I grit out in my most menacing voice.

He gives me a deprecating look, his dark eyes cold and void of emotion. He pulls at me, and I all but fall out of my seat and into his lap, the move unexpected. He holds me tight against him as I struggle to free my arms from his boa constrictor-like grip. "I'm sure a pretty thing like you knows how to use her mouth and body to please a man."

A bit of bile works its way up my throat as I take a deep breath and work on focusing my energy on what I've been taught at kickboxing classes. My nostrils flare as the anger works its way through my body and into my muscles.

"You could be the extra incentive we need to make some of these deals. There are a lot of bored and lonely men in the world who would appreciate your talents."

I jam my head back into his face and hear the distinct crack of his nose. When his grip loosens on me, I clamber off his lap and punch him in the face and then in the stomach until he's doubled over in pain. All my anger comes to a point, and I pummel him, taking out everything on his poor, battered body. He's trying his best to cover his body from my harsh blows, and when he can't stand sitting anymore, he stands, trying to work his way into getting me to stop my attack.

I feel him before I see him. A strong set of arms wraps around my midsection and pulls me away from my assailant, shielding me from view. Clive wipes the blood from his face and spits a tooth out. *Good. Hope that costs a lot to fix!*

"Ethan, glad you're here. Now, you can talk some sense into Addison since giving her this opportunity was your idea."

Are you fucking kidding me?

CHAPTER 38

ETHAN

Oh, fuck no! I pull my fist back and slam it into Clive's face. He goes down like a ton of bricks, and I have to shake the pain out of my hand. I turn to look at Addison and see the unshed tears in her eyes. I reach out to her and pull back at the last second when she flinches.

"Addy, I promise you, he's lying. This was *not* my idea. He called me the other day when you quit and told me to make you take this role or I'd lose my spot as CEO here." She scoffs and shakes her head in disbelief. "I wrote up my resignation letter that day and sent it to Aiden."

The utter look of shock has me stifling my laugh. *Glad to know I can still surprise her.* "I no longer work for *Emulation.*"

She clears her throat and swallows thickly. "What are you going to do?"

"I'm thinking of starting my own company. I'm sure there are a few people here who would love to get out from under the board of directors, and there's plenty of untapped potential around Atlanta."

A set of uniformed officers comes to the door and pushes it

open, startling her. "Miss, are you okay?" one man says, his gun pointed at me. I raise my hands to my head but stay silent and still. I called them when I heard this meeting was happening tonight. I wasn't sure what Clive was going to do, but I figured it was better safe than sorry to get the police here.

She finally nods at the officer's question. "Please, don't point your gun at him. He hasn't hurt me. It's the man on the floor you need."

The cop moves past us to see Clive on the floor, unconscious. He turns to look at us. "Self-defense. He was trying to assault me," she blurts out.

Instinctively, I reach out and wrap my arm around her waist, pulling her to my side. She melts into my embrace for a moment before pushing me away and putting some distance between us.

"We're going to need to get statements from both of you as to what happened here." We both nod as they call for an ambulance for Clive. *What a complete shit show this turned out to be.*

"Where did you learn moves like that?" I ask her when we have a moment alone.

She smirks before her face goes stoic again. "Kickboxing. We make all the girls take classes at the club to protect themselves."

My kick-ass girl. She had this handled even without me. I should have known she could take care of herself. She's been doing it so long on her own.

"Addy, I have a question to ask you." I take a deep breath. "When you were working under Vince at *The Devil's Playground,* were you trafficked?"

She furrows her brows, and her lips turn down into a frown. "Why would you assume I was?"

"Clive called me the other day, the day you resigned, about how you were one of Vince's birdies—his "it" girls. I remember when Vince was killed, and it was on the news all about his money laundering, embezzlement, and how he was also charged with sex trafficking. The girls—your friends, were ya'll being forced into it? Were you *forced* to have sex with me?"

When she shakes her head, relief washes through me. "Vince already had Lia, Everleigh, and Eden under his thumb when I joined the club. He was stopping me from being able to find a job anywhere else. The club... it was my only option." A sad smile spreads across her lips. "Eden kept me safe."

The cop returns, and she closes her mouth, watching as he pulls out a notepad and settles in to ask us both some questions. Addison recounts the events, including the call she received from Clive, asking for the meeting in the first place, and how he attacked her when she told him no.

One of the other board members called me and asked if I knew anything about Addison Snyder and why Clive would want a meeting with her. As soon as I heard he had requested one, I knew it would end badly. I made sure to call the cops when I got into the office, and honestly, I'm lucky the timing worked out how it did.

The cop finishes with our statements, telling us he will be in touch if more information is needed, and then heads out the door. I make no move to get up, and neither does she.

"Tell me more about your time at the club. Let me hear your side of things." She shrugs and shakes her head like it's not important. "Please, Addy, I want to know. You once told me you have a lot of scars. Let me try to help heal some of them."

She takes a deep breath and lets it out as she tucks hair behind her ear. One of her nervous ticks. She tells me about how she got started at the club, and the private shows Vince used to make the girls do. Everything she tells me leads me to believe he would have been fine with these girls being raped if that's what the client wanted.

Eden used to slip roofies to the girls to use in case they ever needed them, or if the men were getting too handsy. According to Addy, she had to use them more than once to get some guy to stop trying to have sex with her.

"Your dad used to ask for me, wanting me to give him private shows. He was close with Vince, and I didn't trust him. One time, after I slept with you, I agreed to give him a lap dance, but that's it. It never went further than that. Although, not for his lack of trying."

I shake my head at my own stupidity. "He showed me pictures of you in his lap. I thought..."

"If there are pictures, it's from that one and *only* time. I don't even know how he could have gotten them. We assumed everything was lost in the fire."

"I have a list of clients you were involved with. How did that get out?"

She shakes her head, a confused look on her face. "I don't know." She shrugs. "When the place burned down, we figured all evidence of the sins there went with it. Eden got a big payout from insurance since she was Vince's only next of kin."

My jaw drops. "Wait a minute, Eden is his daughter?"

She shakes her head. "No, his niece. By marriage. When she got the payout, we girls decided we wanted to open a new club, but we made sure we could keep the girls safe. Everyone has their own reason for coming to work at *RISE*. As long as we can keep them safe and supply them with steady jobs, we've done right by them. No one gets forced into anything they don't want to do, and all the girls take self-defense classes.

"We also vet every one of the members and are highly selective of who we allow through the doors. If someone brings a guest with them, and the guest doesn't follow the rules, the member loses his privileges."

To say I'm impressed would be an understatement. I know Addy has her MBA, but the fact these girls could open such a successful business and have it thriving all these years later is very impressive.

She stands, and I'm shaken out of my stupor. I want to reach out and pull her in for a hug, bury my face in her shoulder and inhale her intoxicating scent. I don't dare touch her, though. I know I no longer have the right to do that.

"I'm so sorry for everything, Addy. I never meant to hurt you the way I did. I don't expect you to be able to forgive me, but I'm hoping for a chance, even if it's just to be your friend. I hope that one day you'll let me into your life again."

She gives me a sad smile and leans down, placing a gentle kiss on my cheek. "Just give me time, Ethan. I'll find you when I'm ready."

She walks out and leaves me alone, sitting in the conference room for the company I used to run. Instead of feeling sorry for myself, I feel the weight of the world has been lifted off my shoulders. I can do whatever I want now. I can run a business *my* way.

CHAPTER 39

ADDISON- 2 MONTHS LATER

I've been working at *RISE* every night for the past two months. I haven't wanted to stop, because when I do, all I think about is Ethan. The feel of his body pressed against mine, his lips, the scruff on his jaw. All of it sends a jolt of pleasure coursing through me.

I haven't gotten laid since him. Even my trusty vibrating friends have started to lose hope of getting me off. It's sad, really, when my battery-operated boyfriend has ceased to please me. No. I need the real thing. The only problem is, I only want it from one man.

Looking out into the crowd, I search for familiar brown eyes, just like I do every night I take the stage. I know he won't be there; his membership was stripped from him, but it doesn't stop me from hoping. The pole is cool under my fingertips as the music comes up, and I start my routine. I seek out random faces, offering a sultry smile as I shake my assets.

I've done the same five routines for so long now, I zone out, my mind seeking solace with Ethan. He's done as I've asked and hasn't tried to contact me, giving me the space I need. I've debated calling him a few times, but as I hover over his number, I chicken out and close out of the app. I don't even know what to say to him.

Yes, I do. I forgive you.

News of him leaving *Emulation* hit the public the next day, and charges against Clive were initiated. Unfortunately, it was a "he said, she said" situation, and he denied he did anything until he was blue in the face. It pays to have good lawyers, but even still, I dragged it out and made him pay a fortune in legal fees before the case was finally dropped.

I haven't heard anything about Ethan's new company. I've tried to research it, but I can't find anything online—or, at least, nothing that ties his name to it. Landry gives me updates here and there, but I try not to ask for them too much. Last I heard, he was doing well. I wanted to ask if Ethan was seeing anyone, but I didn't think my heart could handle it if he said yes, so I let it drop.

The music fades, as do the lights, and I step off the stage and blot my face and neck with a towel. Candy stands next to me with a bright smile on her face.

"Hey, Addy, there are a few gentlemen that want a private show with you."

I shake my head. "I'm not doing private shows anymore, Candy, remember?"

Her face falls, and she shrugs. "I know, but I thought maybe it would help. You've been down so much lately, so I thought you might want the distraction. I'll let them know you aren't interested."

I give her a tight-lipped smile. "I appreciate what you're trying to do. Thank you."

I head down to the main office and pull my mask off. I look around, hoping for some business to attend to, but since I've been putting in so many hours, we are ahead and there really is nothing else I can do at this moment. I open my email and see a job interview request for a small start-up company called *Frameworks*. I've applied to so many jobs in the past few months, I don't even remember applying to this place, but I'm happy to go.

I respond to the message, stating I'd be thrilled to come in and suggest a date and time. Since it's a Sunday, I don't expect to hear back, so when a message comes in a few minutes later, I'm surprised. According to the message, they would be happy to meet with me tomorrow at ten a.m.

I DIG MY KEYS OUT OF MY PURSE AS EDEN POPS HER HEAD OUT OF her door. "Hey, girl," she says.

I turn to look at her and jerk my head in response. "Hey, Eady." I push open the door and lean against it. "What's going on?"

"Just checking on my girl." She looks to the ground and back to me. "Heard from Ethan yet?"

I shake my head. "No. I asked him to give me time, and he's given it to me. Can't blame the guy for listening."

"Lia, Everleigh, and the girls are coming over for a Princess movie night. Want to join us? I bought tons of junk food. Lots of salt and sugar." She smirks. *I'm sure Lia and Everleigh are going to love going home with two sugared-up little girls.*

I smile warmly but shake my head. "Not tonight." I hesitate for a moment. "I have a job interview tomorrow."

I haven't told the girls I've been applying for jobs yet. It took me a few weeks, tons of junk food, cheesy romantic comedies, and my girls to pull me out of my slump. It helps that Eden told me time and time again she would be happy to rip his balls off with her bare hands and shove them down his throat.

She beams. "Addy, that's great. I'm so happy for you."

"Thanks." I let my door close and cross the hall, pulling her into a tight embrace. "Thanks, Eden, for being the best friend I could have found." She hugs me tight, and when we part, she wipes the water under her eyes. "I gotta go." I hook my thumb over my shoulder. "I need to do some research on the place."

"Good luck, girl."

I thank her and head into my apartment for a night of research about *Frameworks.*

I OPEN THE FRONT DOOR TO THE BUILDING AT EXACTLY NINE-fifty and introduce myself to the woman behind the desk before telling her I have a meeting with Don Salvido. The waiting area is small with just a few cushy chairs and a small coffee table between them. I take a seat as I wait for her to get Don for me.

I haven't felt this anxious about a job in a long time. I cross my legs and try to keep my leg from bouncing with nervous energy. I tuck some hair behind my ear and smooth my pencil skirt out. *You've got this, girl.* It's the message I received from Eden this morning, and I keep replaying the words over and over.

The hairs on the back of my neck stand as a familiar scent fills my senses. I jerk my head to the left as Ethan comes into view, a huge smile on his face. Damn, does he look good. He's in a pair of fitted navy chinos and a white button-down shirt with the sleeves rolled to his elbows. His hair is a little longer than it was last time I saw him, but he still looks sexy as hell.

As if any of that would have changed in two months. The man has always been like a Greek god.

"Hi, Addison. Thanks for coming in today."

"I-I," I stammer as I stand on shaky legs. I clear my throat and start over. "I thought I was meeting with Don Salvido. I didn't know you worked here," I say in disbelief.

He gives me one of his huge smiles again. "*Frameworks* is my new company." He waves for me to follow him. "Come on, let's talk in my office."

My legs start moving before I can even wrap my head around it. He leads me to an office and closes the door behind us, motioning for me to take a seat. I look down at where he's indicating and back up at him. "How? I didn't see your name anywhere in my research on this place."

"I've kept my name out of it for now. Since we're a private start-up, no one needs to know. It's better that way."

"Ethan…"

He looks at me, a smile still on his face, but it hasn't reached his eyes. I study him for a moment. He looks tired. So tired. I reach my hand out and touch his cheek. He presses his face into my hand and holds it against him, snuggling into my palm.

"I've missed you so much, Addy. It's been hell staying away from you," he says quietly before dropping my hand and taking a step back.

I don't want him to. I step closer again, as if my body is reaching for his. As if my body knows I belong with him and can't be apart anymore. My heart hammers in my chest, and water fills my bottom lid as I watch him.

"I miss you too, Ethan." I take a deep breath, trying to calm my racing heart. "I've thought of calling you so many times, but I've been too afraid."

He steps into my space and tucks my hair behind my ear,

then gently places his hands on my cheeks to lift my eyes to his chocolate ones. "Afraid of what, baby?" he whispers as if it's a secret among lovers.

"That you've moved on," I whisper back.

He wraps his arms around me and presses my cheek against his chest. "No, baby. Not a chance in hell I'd move on from you." His heart is beating frantically as I wrap my arms around his slender waist. He rubs his hand up and down my back, and a few tears slip free.

"I'm so sorry, Addy. I can't say it enough times." He kisses the top of my head, and for the first time in months, I feel whole again. I've missed him so damn much. He took a piece of me when I pushed him away.

"I forgive you, Ethan."

CHAPTER 40

ETHAN

She fucking forgives me. I'm so happy I think I'll burst. Those three words leaving her sinful lips is like heaven to my ears. I stick my finger under her chin and tilt her head back so she's looking at me, and then my lips come crashing down on hers. My tongue swipes the seam of her lips, and she doesn't hesitate to open for me.

Home. Having her beneath my fingertips, exploring her mouth, it feels like I'm finally coming home after being lost for so long. She moans into the kiss as I walk her backward toward the wall. I press my weight into her and nudge her legs apart to fit mine between us.

When she starts rocking over my leg, I know I need to stop. We aren't doing this here, not like this. I don't want her to think I just need a good fuck, even if I do. I pull back to look into her eyes and smile as her chest heaves.

"I believe you're here for an interview, Ms. Snyder," I tease. She blinks at me a few times before she finally nods, and I allow her to step away from the wall. "Have a seat and we can discuss why you want this job."

She smiles and shakes her head. She would have to be an idiot to know she's not a shoo-in already. The role is for a marketing position. Where she has worked with the other girls to make *RISE* so successful over the years, and she was always good with clients at *Emulation,* it would be the perfect position for her.

She didn't even apply for the job. I created a fake email address and sent her an interview request. I know she has been looking for a job lately; Aiden told me after they went out for drinks last week. He's leaving *Emulation* to come work for me, too, but I made him promise not to tell her. I know they were close.

I managed to drag a lot of old employees with me, but that's another reason I need to keep my name out of things —for now. It's better if the board doesn't know I'm stealing employees until it's too late for them to do anything about it.

I go through the motions of telling her what the job entails, asking about her experience, and where she sees herself in a few years. All the standard questions. Then I open it to her to ask anything she wants to know.

"Are you the one who sent the email to bring me here to this interview?"

I grin wide and nod. "A little birdy told me you have been looking for a job, and I knew we had the perfect position here for you... if you want it, of course."

"I'm going to kill Aiden," she mumbles as she shakes her head. Her cheeks flame under my gaze. "I've been waiting for you to seek me out at the club."

"They revoked my membership. I'm sure if one of the owners would vouch for me, though, I could get back in their good graces to be able to see a show."

"You're not mad?"

I shake my head. "*RISE* is part of who you are, part of what made you. I won't take that from you."

"What are the rules here on interoffice dating?" she asks with a sly smirk.

"Allowed. Why? Is there someone who works here you are interested in?" I tease.

She stands and walks behind the desk, stopping between my spread legs. She reaches her fingers down and runs them through my hair. I close my eyes and relish in the feeling of her fingers as they dance over my scalp, a quiet hum of appreciation leaving my lips. I lift my hands to her hips, holding her in place, and open my eyes to look at her again.

"Can we start over?" she asks. I see the fear of rejection in her eyes as she bites her lip and waits for my reply.

I stand, towering over her petite frame again. "You're mine, Addison Snyder. No more running. We're in this together, the good and bad. I promise to talk to you if I have any doubts in my mind."

"Do you really want me to work here with you?"

"Addy, I don't ever want you to leave my side again." My eyes grow heated as I watch her closely. "If I had my way, I'd tie you to the bed and never let you leave."

"Is that so, Mr. Freeman?" she asks, wrapping her arms around my neck, pulling my face closer to hers.

"Addy, the things I want to do to you would require it. You'd be trying to get away from the overload of pleasure."

Her breathing hitches, and her cheeks flush, but those are the only indications she's turned on. She's always been good at hiding her arousal unless she wants me to know.

"What's the offer? For the job. Give me your best pitch, and I might consider it." She pushes me down into my seat and climbs into my lap, her skirt pulling tight over her hips. I lean forward, trying to press my lips to hers, and she holds me back with her finger over my mouth.

"Brat." I bite her finger playfully. "Be my marketing manager. You have free rein to hire your own team."

"Okay, and what about compensation and benefits? Benefits are a huge part of the job, you know." She teases me by pressing her core against me and rubbing herself along my growing bulge."

I groan and drop my head back on my chair. "I'll give you orgasms every day, and we can even work on some more of those office fantasies you have yet to tell me about. I can't wait to try them all out."

"If I didn't know better, Ethan, I'd say you do this with all the ladies."

"Not a chance in hell, babe, only you. And I'm going to marry you one day to prove it. You're it for me, Addy. I want you and only you. Take the job, move in with me, and make me the happiest man alive. Please, baby? I love you so much. I can't picture my life without you in it."

She takes a deep breath, and it looks like she's going to cry again. It's the first time I've been able to tell her in person how I truly feel about her. I love her. I want the whole damn world to know it, too. When I know she's ready, I'm going to put a ring on her finger and give her the wedding of her dreams. Then, I want to have a million kids with her.

As if she can read my mind, she laughs. "I love you, too, Ethan. So damn much."

I dig my fingers through her hair and pull her lips to mine for a bruising kiss.

Addison Snyder is finally mine.

EPILOGUE

ADDISON 3 MONTHS LATER

Us girls are all sitting at my new kitchen table as Ethan, Landry, and Luca lift heavy boxes and carry them into the house. Lia and Everleigh's little girls are playing together in the living room. Watching these men work like this is turning me on, and you can bet when I get Ethan alone, he's going to be one very happy man.

I can't believe I'm finally moving in with him. *Correction, he finally convinced me to move in with him.* I may have been playing a bit of hardball, not wanting to leave my apartment and leave Eden in this building alone. She's the last of us now to be here full-time, and it sucks. I want her to be happy. If she would just open her heart, I know she would find the right man.

Ethan comes back in and steals a kiss from me, and Landry smacks him upside the head.

"I want to get out of here at *some* point today. Stop sucking face with her," he chastises.

Ethan is now like one of the family, but it took a long time for him to smooth things over with the girls. Everleigh threatened to castrate him only about a hundred times before she would finally show him her softer side and welcome him into the group. I'm sure he had to make all sorts of promises, including chopping off his own dick if he ever messes up like that again.

Lia was much easier to win over as Landry had a hand in making her see reason. I'm sure that consisted of a million orgasms. Not that I blame her. Who wouldn't want that kind of promise? He's even managed to become close with Luca, and the three guys hang out pretty regularly, which makes it easy for us girls to still hang out all the time.

That leaves Eden. I look over at her, and she smiles at me, but I still see the tension there. She knows how I feel about Ethan, and she knows he's not perfect. She's willing to give him another chance because I'm giving him another chance. That's all I could ask of her. Now, she just needs to let us play matchmaker and set her up. I wonder what Ethan's friend Callan is up to? They seemed to have a good time at the charity ball...

The guys get the final boxes downstairs and come up to collect us. Landry scoops Aliana up in his arms and blows a raspberry on her belly. She squeals in delight and holds his cheeks between her little hands, and he smiles warmly at her and gives her a kiss on the nose.

Luca picks up Rory and pulls her against him. She drops her head on his shoulder and yawns, wrapping her arms around his neck. "Looks like someone needs a nap."

"No," she starts to whine and move in his grasp. He strokes the back of her head, and she settles down again, closing her eyes. She's going to be asleep before he even reaches the elevator.

Ethan wraps his arm around my waist and pulls me to his

side. "Thanks so much for all the help, guys. It would have taken us all day to load and unload the truck. There's a game next weekend. How about we have a cookout here?"

The guys agree while we girls roll our eyes at the men. "Y'all better not forget about the women in your lives in favor of sports," Everleigh says, placing her hands on her hips.

"Everyone's invited. It'll be a good time," Ethan says.

"Besides, Evergreen, you know I could never forget about you. Even if I wanted to, you'd kick my ass into submission." Luca kisses her on her temple and smiles wide at the rest of us, his hand absentmindedly rubbing her belly where their twins are rapidly growing.

"All right, everyone, get out of here so Ethan and I can christen every room in our new house," I say, pushing them toward the door.

"You've spent more time here in the past few months than you have at your apartment. I'm pretty sure you've already taken care of that," Eden says as she quirks her eyebrow in question.

I blush but push them all toward the door, waving bye and hugging my girls. I close the door and lock it, not needing a random interruption.

I lean against the door and look around at all the boxes we have to unpack. He already had the furniture, so we put a few pieces in storage that I'm not ready to part with, especially if we get a bigger place. The rest I sold or donated. All that's left are my personal belongings.

He smiles at me as he stalks over, his eyes heated. I lick my suddenly dry lips as I watch his muscles move under his snug shirt. He presses me against the door, and I feel his growing bulge between my legs.

"Do you have any idea how hard it was to keep my hands

off you today? Especially when you're wearing those snug yoga pants and no panties?"

"How do you know I'm not wearing any panties?" I ask, running my hands over his body.

He dips his fingers past the waistband of my pants and runs his fingers through my slick folds. I drop my head back and close my eyes in pleasure.

"Because I know how dirty you are, baby, and I know how much you like to torture me." He pulls his hand away suddenly. "I left you a present on the bed. Go change, and I'll be there in a few."

Butterflies dance in my belly as he gives me space to move around him, and I walk to the bedroom. Laying on the bed is a new bra and panty set, along with a mask. Ethan's membership was reinstated at *RISE*, and we've gone there a few times together so he can watch me perform. Afterward, we head back home for a private show. I have a few masks here still because I keep forgetting to take them back. We never use my room there anymore; we always come here.

He's met my Aunt Linda and Uncle Bill now a few times, and they adore him. He wanted me to try to mend things between them since they are the only family I have, and I'm so happy he pushed me to do that. We're getting along really well.

A few Sundays a month, we get together with his mom, sisters, brother-in-law, Donnie, and his nephew, Stevie. His mom is so happy to have all her kids come to visit and always makes me feel welcome. I love her as I would my own mom, and I'm so happy to have her in my life.

He comes into the room a few minutes later, my mind still taking a trip down memory lane when he looks at me.

"Hello, Madam Ember," he says, his voice husky with need.

I pull the mask down over my eyes and turn to face him.

"You hired me for a private show. Do you want me to dance?" I ask, repeating the first words I ever spoke to him.

"Do you want to dance?" he challenges.

I smile and push him down on the bed, straddling his hips. "It's going to be a long night, Mr. Freeman. I hope you can handle it."

"As long as I'm with you, I can handle anything, baby."

NOTE FROM ME

Holy heck! What a wild ride, huh? Are you scratching your head though wondering why I didn't wrap up a few key points with a pretty little bow? Plot items such as the fire actually being arson? Or who the hell Al Costanza is??

Good news is ALL will be sorted out and you will get the answers you seek…but you need to pick up the last book in the series, *Marked by Sin* to get those answers.

Check out the blurb and a sneak peek of *Marked by Sin* by Shanna Swenson, and get a glimpse of Eden and Callan's steamy story.

Marked by Sin premieres
March 13, 2021
PREORDER NOW

By day, I, Eden Riser, am a timid librarian.

By night, I becomes Madam Roxie, superstar of the gentlemen's club I'm the owner of—RISE.

This is my story…

All my sisters now have their happily ever afters, just like the novels I tend to wrap myself in to escape the scars of my past. I know love will never find me. Not that I even deserve it… But deep down, I still want it. Quietly hiding behind a mask and glasses these past ten years has been easy for this ruined soul with enough sinful skeletons to fill a whole closet. The problem is that it's getting harder and harder for me to keep my feelings hidden…and to keep my two identities separate— even if it's been as much for safety as for anonymity. Especially when larger-than-life public figure and celebrity book model, Callan Manning enters the picture.

   Will unraveling secrets be what destroys us both or is love strong enough to pardon even my darkest sins?

CALLAN MANNING

Yeah, I'm a public figure who takes more selfies of my biceps than I probably should. But this narcissist has a big heart hidden beneath my bulky frame. I'm a caregiver for my nephew with cerebral palsy, and I love my life, but something is missing…

The minute I saw Roxie on that stage, I knew I had to have her, in whatever way I could. But her idea of sexual torment took me to a whole new level of submission I wasn't accustomed to. There are parts of her that remain untouchable, and God, do I want to touch…

Thing is, I also want another woman, too; a woman who drives me as insane as Roxie does but is her polar opposite in every way—Eden. Something doesn't add up here, though. I know those eyes, I've seen them before. I'll figure this mystery out if it's the last thing I do.

———

Marked by Sin premieres
March 13, 2021
PREORDER NOW

SNEAK PEEK AT MARKED BY SIN BY SHANNA SWENSON

EDEN

I sigh as I get out of my monster of a truck that morning. It's been ten years. Ten long, bittersweet years without him. Marco. My rock. My first love. My dark knight. The emptiness I felt following his death still hasn't left me, and hits me especially hard today, the anniversary of that awful day. The day he sacrificed himself for me. The day he destroyed my enemy. The day we burned down *The Devil's Playground*. The day the caged birdies flew free from their bonds.

The vivid memories of that night come barreling into me this morning as I remember the pit that swallowed me whole, the vortex of emotion once I realized what Marco planned to do to free me. What he'd meant when he said Cordelia had to die, for it was him who had to die beside her in order to save me from the Devil himself. And yet we still weren't safe—*aren't* safe! It was false security because there are still people we're hiding from...

I smile now as I look up at the four-sided brick building that has been my escape these last many years—my library, Walters Regional Library, where I work as the library manager.

I recall the fated day that Addison stopped me from taking my own life and how close her, Everleigh, Lia, and I all are. I don't know where I would be without my girls, my sisters.

Almost as if reading my thoughts, my phone buzzes with text messages.

Lia: *I love you, I'm here if you wanna talk.*

Ev: *Stay strong, you bad-ass phoenix.*

Then my phone rings and I answer it, smiling as I see that Addy's calling me.

I answer with, "Hey, lady."

"You doing ok today, sis?" Addison's soft voice asks me.

"I'm hanging in there."

"I know today's gonna be a tough one for you. You working today?"

"Yeah, you?"

"Me too. We have a meeting I'm not looking forward to."

"Man, I'm sorry."

"Don't be. At least I have a good view. Hot boss and all." She giggles.

I can't help but grin. Her "hot boss" is Ethan Freeman, who also happens to be her boyfriend. "Well, don't work too hard, girl. Thanks for checking in on me. I'll see you later tonight." I hang up the phone.

Crap! I see Samantha Zeller, AKA up-and-coming fantasy author Sam D. Zeller, standing at the door to the library. "Oh, jeez, I apologize."

I forgot today is her talk here and I'm running late on this Thursday morning.

"No worries," she states as I move to the door and unlock it.

I hurry to flip the lights on and throw my bag surreptitiously on the counter, then turn to her and extend my hand.

"It's a pleasure to finally meet you, Ms. Zeller. I'm Eden Riser. I'm a big fan of yours."

"Oh, really?" Samantha asks, surprised. "I'm flattered, truly. Thanks so much for having me here today."

She's lovely, brown hair and blue eyes, clad in a gray dress suit with a cream silk blouse and red pumps.

"Of course. The library loves to support its local authors." I give her a big smile and she returns it.

"Well, it means a lot to an indie like myself. Every avenue helps."

"Where do you want these, Sam?" comes a rough voice and as I look up to the face behind it, I freeze.

Callan Manning stands there, his big, tattooed biceps holding an overflowing box of books. He's as gorgeous as he was the last time I saw him, the night of the charity ball I went to with Addy and Ethan—and Cal as my date. In person, he's larger than life, as entrancing as he is on every book cover I've ever seen him—and his Instagram page that I stalk like a fat kid drooling over cake. His brown hair is close cut, spiked with some gel, his jaw is thickly bearded and his tight navy polo and denim jeans fit like a glove. But it's his sparkling blue eyes that hold me captive. My heart is hammering in my chest, and I feel my jaw dropping as they suddenly take me in.

That night comes rushing back to me. God, it's been over a year ago but I remember it like it was yesterday. Dancing, dining, and laughing with him. Him holding me close, the feel of that solid body firm against my own. Gah, I felt like Cinderella and he was a perfect gentleman, walking me to my door and kissing the back of my hand. That night I was "Roxanne," some random, masked companion. Simply an alluring arm toy for a man like him. He'd not asked to come in and I hadn't invited him to; for a few reasons, one being my fear of intimacy, but the main being that I didn't wanna burst that perfect bubble I was floating in that night, even if I'm positive Ethan demanded Cal behave himself, come hell or high water.

"Hey there," Cal says, and I'm completely speechless. I know I'm totally fan-girling right now, but I can't help myself, I'm still completely smitten with this gorgeous stud of a man, who despite his image on Sam's cover, surprises me with his presence here today.

"Ms. Riser," I hear Samantha say, and she turns towards me.

"Oh, umm..." *Shit, get a grip on yourself, Eden.* "Right this way."

I turn, tearing my eyes from Callan's enticing tall, broad frame.

I hear his heavy footfalls behind me as I lead him down the hallway and open another door with a key, walking in and throwing on the switch as I blushingly show him a table and podium that's set up for the talk.

"Right here, Mr. Manning."

He smirks, unsurprised that I know who he is—as if I couldn't.

"Call me Cal," he says and extends his hand after he's set the box down; he makes it look feather light.

"Eden." I take his hand gently, feeling my heart leap into my throat as his big palm interlocks with mine. Funny, it did the same thing the night of the ball.

"Wow, that's a beautiful name."

"Thank you." *And you're a beautiful man.*

"Cal," I hear Samantha say, coming through the door. I drop Callan's hand like it's a hot plate and look to Samantha. "I see you've met my brother," she says to me with a smile. "Cal, I'm gonna go grab Caleb and Sally."

Callan nods at her and gives me another crooked smile; I swear to God my panties are soaked now. I've forgotten that he's a walking, talking orgasm. "So, you recognized my biceps." His voice drops, laced with superiority, and *Poof!* My bubble bursts just as quickly as it encased me.

Now I remember why I hate men—all conniving, manipulative men—with a passion as heated as a hot July day here in Atlanta, Georgia. My smile fades and my logical, sarcastic self takes over; my invisible mask suddenly covers my face, hiding me well.

"I recognized your eyes," I retort and turn on my heel. "If you'll excuse me, I need to get the library ready for the morning. Feel free to set up as you wish, and let me know if you need anything."

"Sorry, didn't realize you were a lesbian," he mumbles under his breath.

"Excuse me?" I whip around, my brows furrowed.

"You heard me," he smarts.

"I'm not even going to *dignify* that with an answer."

"Ok, whatever."

I roll my eyes. "Are you always so incorrigible?"

"I don't even know what that word means." He leans back against the table and props his hips there, looking far too comfortable in his skin, despite that he's just confessed he's not the most intelligent man in the world—not that he has to be, with a face and body like that.

"Sounds like you need to spend more time in the library then, Mr. Manning," I sass.

"Sounds like *you* need to spend more time under a real man." He raises a brow, and I close my eyes in annoyance and walk off.

I begin turning the computers on, clock in, and throw my new brown leather Michael Kors purse into the drawer I keep it in behind the front counter. I hear the automatic doors open and look up to see the cutest little boy, along with Samantha and an elderly woman, coming toward me in a power wheelchair. He favors Callan, and immediately I wonder if this child is his. He gives me a bright beaming smile, and I melt right in my chair. I stand and return it, speaking first. "Well, hello there, handsome."

He lets out a small wail, in an attempt to communicate, that sweet smile returning and my heart feels like it might just explode with emotion for this precious, physically-disabled child with an innocence as endearing as his smile.

"This is my son, Caleb," Samantha states as they stop in front of the counter.

"Hi, Caleb. I'm Eden. It's good to meet you. Are you a big fan of books?" I ask.

"Oh, he *loves* books. Especially when we do the voices," says the white-haired lady who comes to a stop behind him. She gives me a warm smile. "I'm Sally."

"Eden. Welcome to Walters Regional Library. Please, come in and get cozy."

Sally's smile widens, and I'm at ease with these people...until I hear Callan's voice.

"Sis, where the hell do you want this banner set up?"

"Callan, *language*, you aren't a child. I shouldn't have to tell you these things," Samantha grumbles and walks toward the conference room.

I shake my head—*what an imbecile*. I should have known!

Callan Manning is the face of Samantha's book covers and, who am I kidding, the body too. Her latest book is a gorgeous fantasy novel entitled *Made for Glory* with Callan; face covered by a spartan-type helmet, his huge biceps thrusting a massive sword into the mud, clad in only a cloth that drapes around his hips, covering his man-parts. His eyes pierce one's soul as the blue orbs stare back at you. A vibrant lightning bolt strikes in the background. I've stared at this cover far too many times, entranced by those eyes, and overcome with lust for that big, muscled body of his. To say I'm obsessed is an understatement. I check his social media pages every single day, multiple times a day. It's pathetic, I know, but after the pure hell my uncle put me through on a daily basis for years, I'm fucked up. Possibly beyond all repair. And although men are now my play-things and I want nothing more than to control them, and I *do* in my club, I still enjoy the male physique and lust after it. And a face, eyes, and body like Callan Manning's is easy to get overcome by.

I try to shake my disappointment away; I had this image in my head of how great he was in person. I mean, he *was* great in person—last time I met him. I couldn't have asked for a more charming prince charming but this guy... Well, needless to say, that sparkling image is gone, and my stomach burns sourly with annoyance, disillusionment, and pain. He's just like every other man I've ever known since Marco; he's not special at all.

Sounds like I need to send out an invitation to my club so I can break him down at the knees. Hmm... Roxie's *exactly* what a man like Callan Manning needs.

CALLAN

DAMN, THE LIBRARIAN IS A SMOKING HOT FOX. TALL, CURVES that go on for days, and plump, red lips that I imagine wrapped around my big johnson.

I give her a wink as I place Sam's books back into the box then lick my lips as she pushes her glasses back up her nose. I entertain a fantasy of fucking her right here on this desk with *only* those sexy red frames on. It would be so easy to spread those long legs and jerk that clip from her hair. Man, if I'm not sporting a boner in a library. There's something so taboo about that.

Sheesh, get a grip, Manning, I tell myself, but there's something so familiar about her. I feel like I know her. I've seen her before... That voice, I know I've heard its pitch somewhere prior to today.

I ponder as I haul the final box back to my truck, then turn to head back inside to see what else my sister needs help with only to stop as she and the librarian are exiting the front doors.

"Thank you so much, Ms. Riser. It was truly a pleasure."

"Just Eden, please. The pleasure is all mine, I assure you, Samantha."

Eden. Wow, that name is so sexy, like her, and I grin as she shakes Sam's hand.

Caleb and Sally went on back home after about an hour. He got his books and was good to go, plus Sally had promised Caleb ice cream, so he was eager for that.

I take a bag from Sam and pull it to my shoulder, watching the librarian lock up for the day. I can't believe we closed it down, but Sam had lots of visitors and despite that it was a success, I can see she's exhausted.

"I look forward to seeing you soon," Eden says.

"Likewise. I'll be in touch." Sam waves and approaches me.

"Good to meet you, Eden," I say and give her a nod. Her lips pucker and her brow raises but I get no verbal response. *Good going, ass-wipe, she hates you.*

Then I stop dead in my tracks as I watch her walking to my right, to a brand-new, jacked-up, blacked out GMC Sierra. No fucking way that's hers... is it?

"Uh, Eden?" I ask because I just can't help myself. I gotta know... "That your truck?"

The devilish smirk on her gorgeous face is a stark contrast to her heavenly name. "Sure is."

Well, stuff my ass and call me a turkey! I'll be damned. I know I'm gaping, but I'm utterly stupefied, and as this sexy dame hops up on the nerf bar and opens the truck door, I'm drooling all over myself.

"That is one sexy as *fuck* vehicle, m'lady."

She has the nerve to grin and winks as she says, "Eat your heart out, stud."

By God, I think I just met the woman I want to marry.

PREORDER MARKED BY SIN NOW

ABOUT CARA WADE

Cara Wade is a daydreamer, and a lifelong teenybopper...boy bands forever! She would love to spend the day in the kitchen baking up sweet treats, but hates doing the dishes after. When she is not writing (or suffering writer's block) you can find her reading, hiking, or relaxing by the water. She lives in northern Massachusetts with her loving husband and the newest edition to her family, her baby boy.